PEPPERTREE LANE

Jean Delaney was very grateful to her Uncle
Gerald, who had given her and her mother and
young brother a home – but Gerald's foster-
son Rob was convinced that the whole family
were out to make all they could out of the old
man. Was he right to be suspicious?

PEPPERTREE LANE

by

LINDEN GRIERSON

MILLS & BOON LIMITED
17-19 FOLEY STREET
LONDON W1A 1DR

First published 1956
This edition 1974

ISBN 0 263 71601 5

Made and Printed in Great Britain by
C. Nicholls & Company Ltd,
The Philips Park Press, Manchester

CHAPTER ONE

STREAKS of brilliant colour, too fantastic for any artist's palette, began to stain the sky in the west where high banks of clouds lost their look of remote white purity and became in a matter of seconds something from an inferno. Some were tipped finely with gold, others with purple, and the pale blue of the late afternoon faded into orange pink and yellow, flinging into sharp relief the silhouettes of the gum trees bordering the wide long paddocks. The placid river, away from the cool shadows of the high banks, reflected the changing and deepening colours of the sky; occasionally as a fly or an insect skimmed the water the reflections became distorted and would shimmer like a coloured cascade.

The solitary occupant of the utility did not glance upwards or sideways to marvel at a picture no human being could paint with truth and justice, he pulled his hat down further over his eyes to lessen the glare of the sun and did a wild turn, after scraping through the last of the gates, to come to a wheezy halt beside a battered gate which had once been painted green. It was many years since a paintbrush of any description had even been wafted in its direction, the elements, principally the sun, had cracked and blistered the original coat and colour beyond all recognition. The wire fence was torn in places and had been patched sufficiently to keep out sheep and other animals, huge lantana bushes sprawled untidily, a mass of bright colour on either side of the gate and the whole large garden was surrounded by spreading peppertrees, their light green leaves hanging motionless in the evening air.

The young man who alighted slowly from the utility did not notice the condition of the wooden gate as it was pushed open, neither did he give any indication of hearing the loud protesting squeak as it swung to behind him. The squeak was a signal for the man sitting on the veranda to open his eyes and he grunted a greeting as the other idly pushed aside the swinging tendrils of the grapevine as he came up the veranda steps to join him, he flung his wide-brimmed hat, which was slightly green in places with age and generously splashed elsewhere with spots of oil, with unerring accuracy on to a low cane chair. Its owner sank back on his haunches beside the elder man who looked at him quizzically.

"Sell 'em?" inquired the occupant of the chair briefly.

"I did."

"Good price?"

"Naturally. As usual, you timed it well. You'll be a millionaire one of these days, Pop."

The prospective millionaire snorted. "They were good lambs," he said as though that explained everything, and looked reflectively across the thick grass which was the lawn over the hedge to the nearest of the paddocks where the shadows were lengthening swiftly. "And there's plenty more."

The younger man laughed, showing two rows of perfect white teeth.

"No need to part with them yet, surely? The cheque for today's lot will keep the wolf from the door for many months to come."

The brief conversation lasted them a long time. The elder man continued to stare out across his land, relaxed after a hard day's work, and the younger one reached out a hand, pulled a bunch of green grapes from the thick vine and still sitting on the bare wooden floor of the veranda, munched contentedly. As the silence lengthened he turned his head to look with affection at his companion and saw a man in his late fifties with a thick mop of grey hair and grey bushy eyebrows which overhung a pair of keen blue eyes. Beneath these there were many wrinkles on the brown

6

leathery skin, some caused naturally by his age, others by the continuous glare of the sun and the outdoor life he led.

Most people in the district called Gerald Delaney a mean, stingy old man. He drove a hard bargain, carefully checked all his bills and refused to pay a halfpenny for something he had not bought. If he was not so tight-fisted, they argued, why did he not have something done to the old homestead which looked as if it was falling to pieces around his ears, why did he persist in running about the countryside in either the old utility or that ancient car which looked, and sounded, as though it was held together with pieces of wire? Others would look at the latest acquisition in the huge machinery shed and wonder, for in there, carefully tended by a man brought from Sydney specifically for the job, were the tractors and the headers, the ploughs and other farm machinery, all clean and brightly painted. Still others, who knew more but dared not say so, thought of the cheques which had saved so many from financial disasters, they thought of those who had suffered bereavement or the loss of a home by fire and wondered at the way they faced the world afterwards, seemingly better off than they had been before. Only the bank manager knew for certain what transpired, and he loved and admired the man who so willingly helped those in need but who stubbornly refused to allow himself to be referred to or recognised as a public benefactor.

Sometimes, as he signed those cheques which would bring comfort to some deserving person, Gerald Delaney, more commonly and popularly known as Pop, would stare across the room into the sunshine. He had only Rob, the son of the one woman he had loved in his youth and who now lived with him, Rob who was well provided for under the terms of his father's will and who had added to it so carelessly during the past few years; there was little he could give Rob now, so he might just as well part with it this way, he argued as he blotted his signature.

Rob Fraser, glancing occasionally at his companion as he kept popping grapes into his mouth, kept thinking on these things, and only when it was quite dark did he make a move. He stretched out his legs in front of him, leaned back against the wall of the house behind him and put his hands lazily behind his head.

"By the way, Pop, Bill was asking if you'd received his letter – he wanted to know about that lucerne you had for sale."

"Don't know. Haven't opened the mail bag yet."

"And it's been here three days!"

"No hurry."

"You ought to be ashamed of yourself," Rob smiled as he got to his feet. "There may be something important in the bag –"

"Such as?"

"More cheques, for instance. Invitations –"

"To what?"

"You're being extremely awkward tonight, Pop!"

"Merely getting hungry. You open the mail bag, boy." He resumed his contemplation of the world beyond his feet.

Rob looked at him, smiled again and went into the house to switch on the lights and begin the usual search for the mail bag. It was eventually discovered in the bread bin where it had been carelessly thrown with three loaves of bread, still wrapped in the paper in which they had been delivered. Rob grimaced a little as he unwrapped the loaves and noticed patches of mould on the brown crusts. These should have been given to the station cook, but no doubt Pop had forgotten them and Sam had not bothered to inquire where they were, which accounted for the staleness of the bread they had been eating of late.

Opening the mail bag, he sorted the contents. There were papers, days old now, circulars, bills, receipts and a

8

few sealed letters which he carried through on to the veranda. The sudden glare of the light made Pop blink, but he did not move or appear much interested when the bundle of letters were dropped from above his head to fall in a cascade on to his lap.

"Who wrote all this lot?" he demanded to know. "Hope none need answering. Hate writing letters! Where's dinner?"

"Should be ready any time now."

"Sam gets worse. No idea of time at all," he grumbled. "Sometimes wish we had a housekeeper."

Rob laughed at the thought of it. "Until he comes you may as well fill in the intervening time by looking at your correspondence," he suggested, reaching for another bunch of grapes.

"You'll have belly ache," observed Pop, turning the letters over one by one, then a thick-set finger was inserted under the flaps and the contents of each were withdrawn and carefully perused. Pop missed nothing, then he flung them down beside his chair. Only one brought forth any comment, he read it through twice and raised his head.

"This is from Marie," he announced.

"And who's she?"

"My sister-in-law. You've heard me mention her, surely."

"Never." Rob shook his head.

"Thought I'd told you. Anyway, old Fred's dead."

"And who's old Fred?"

"Young brother of mine." He paused for a moment and the younger man looked for signs of grief, but Pop's face was expressionless. "We hadn't much in common, he was younger than me. Poor Fred." He did pause thoughtfully. "Always felt sorry for his wife. Always Yes, Fred. No, Fred. Although she hadn't much backbone. Fred called her placid. I didn't. She was afraid of him, he ruled the roost and no mistake. Two youngsters, boy and girl." That was the history of the other part of the Delaney family, thought Rob with a grin as the other tapped the letter with his finger. "She writes to ask if she can come here –"

"What on earth for?" Rob spun round to stare at the letter.

"Home isn't theirs. Fred died suddenly and left debts. The daughter's working but not earning sufficient to keep three. Sound a bit destitute. Marie offers to housekeep in return for a roof over their heads. Funny, just said I sometimes wished we had a housekeeper."

"It's ridiculous!" exclaimed Rob.

"Why is it?"

"We don't want women and children out here!"

"No, we don't," agreed Pop slowly, and glanced at the letter again. "The children, perhaps, but not Marie. Although, in all fairness, I must say I don't know her very well." He frowned, glancing once more at his watch; both that and his stomach informed him it was past meal time. "Here, read it. Tell me what you think."

Rob read the closely written pages swiftly and a frown gathered between his fine eyes. It struck him chiefly as a begging letter. The stress was laid rather heavily upon the dire straits in which Marie Delaney and her two children had been left, for her husband had evidently lived up to his income during his lifetime and had given no thought to what might happen to his family in the event of his sudden death. There were sentences which annoyed him as he read them. "Fred always said you would be willing to help us, and if you can't, Gerald, perhaps you could suggest something." It was obvious what was to be suggested. "Fred always made the decisions, I don't know what to do. It's impossible to stay here and I know living is cheaper in the country. Jean wasn't very keen about me writing to you, but you're Fred's only relative and her uncle, she's working in the city, but it's a big strain on her, having to keep us all."

10

"Who's Jean?" Rob inquired.

"The daughter."

"Oh! To my mind this contains a heap of insinuations! Fred, who by the way, doesn't seem to be much mourned – how long ago did this happen?" He skimmed the pages again. "A couple of months, evidently. Fred thought he knew something, I don't like this sentence. 'He often told me you weren't without a penny or two–'"

Pop chuckled rather grimly. "You don't know Marie. She puts things badly, for he always took the words out of her mouth and she had to be content to let him do so."

"Here's another sentence. 'I believe Peppertree Lane is a large house, we would look after it for you and help with your entertaining.' Ha!" Rob handed the letter back. "No," he said forcibly. "They hope to come out here and live in luxury for the rest of their lives. They think that with all your money they'll have a fine time. I don't like it, Pop," he added as the other looked at him and then waved his arms to embrace the veranda and the lighted rooms beyond. "Besides, is this the sort of place to invite city women to?"

"What's wrong with it?"

"It's never tidy for a start –"

"Half the mess is yours," protested Pop energetically.

"Whether it's mine or not, it's untidy. It's always been this way and we like it so!"

"Too right we like it this way!"

"If they came they would probably change everything," said Rob, moodily, thinking of a woman's hand moving all his belongings. "Don't do it, Pop. Send them money if you like, write and say you're sorry to learn of your brother's demise and leave it at that. They haven't bothered with you before this happened, you've never mentioned a family to me before, so why do they do it now?"

"Because of Fred's sudden demise."

"Precisely. And here's Sam with the dinner."

11

"Not before time either," said Pop, getting to his feet and leading the way into the large dining-room. They had their meals here because it was near to the veranda where they spent most of their time, sitting near together at one end of the long mahogany table.

As he waded through the plate piled high with roast mutton, boiled potatoes, pumpkin and beans, Gerald Delaney was thinking of his brother, the brother's wife and the children. He and Fred, who was ten years younger, had never had anything in common; the difference in their ages had been too wide a bridge to cover in their childhood. Fred had been slightly built and rather weak and had resented his brother's fine physique. The inferior feeling had made him defend himself against imaginary wrongs by the use of his tongue and at times that could sting. Fred liked the city, his brother did not. Fred also liked Marie, and thinking of her, Pop hesitated with his fork half way to his mouth. A tiny woman – she had to be; Fred would not choose one who was taller or more robustly built than he was himself – she was hesitant, nervy and so dependent on others, in fact she was all the things Pop disliked in a woman. So different from the girl who had been Rob's mother. Even after all these years his eyes softened at the thought of her. She had been his only love, the light of his life, even if she had never been his. Robert Fraser had been the lucky one, for a few years at least, then he too had gone and left his child in the care of his best friend, the man who loved him because he was the son of Elizabeth.

Pop thought of the children. The boy he had never seen, for he had been born after his own last visit to Melbourne, was it ten or eleven years since he had paid an unexpected call upon his family? Eleven years. The girl had been a tiny little thing, rather sweet in her ways but very quiet; he had thought her subdued by her father's domineering attitude.

12

Another forkful of mutton was placed in his mouth and he grimaced.

"Marie might be a better cook than Sam," he murmured.

"Still thinking about that?" came the snappish answer.

"And why not?" Pop put down the fork and pushed his plate away. "After all, they are my relatives and I should help if I can –"

Rob could almost see the workings of the old man's mind. Marie was his sister-in-law, her children were his nephew and niece, the natural heirs to all Gerald Delaney possessed. If they had no one else it was only right they should turn to him as the only other member of the family for help. Such an appeal would not go amiss with such a man either. When he had read the letter he had known it would touch the softness of Pop's heart, but he did not wish him to act on impulse and regret it afterwards.

"Promise me you'll think it over very carefully before you do anything," he pleaded earnestly. "They're complete strangers and might be terrors to live with! Remember they're city folk, so different from us; they've lived where there have been all the conveniences, hot and cold water on tap, a decent bathroom and a modern kitchen. You know what some of those homes are like. All chrome and pale paint! They've had transport at their doorstep, shops near at hand, theatres, beaches, they've everything we haven't got here."

Pop helped himself to a bunch of grapes and began to pick them one by one from the stalk.

"We've more here than they've ever had down there," he stated flatly. "We've a beach. Don't tell me we haven't. You've been swimming there for years. We've sunshine. Plenty of fresh air. Milk, good milk, straight from the cow. Fruit. Clear water –"

"From a five-thousand-gallon tank," murmured Rob.

13

"We've roads. *You* can get into Murra Creek in record time on 'em anyway! We also have the telephone. Mail three times a week. A house that's a heck of a size for two. Kitchen with an oven big enough to roast a bullock –"

"And which makes said kitchen something Dante never dreamed about!"

"Never met the feller," said Pop innocently. "Who was he?"

Rob was laughing. "Go on with your list of advantages."

"We've everything to make a child happy," said the other seriously. "It's the *children* I'm thinking about, son. Not Marie. We'll have to put up with her if we want the other two. Imagine the fun the boy will have here. His own horse. Pets by the dozen –"

"He might be a weakling and have no desire to have horses and pets," retorted Bob scathingly. "Besides, there's no school." And don't suggest you send him to college, he thought suddenly. That would never do!

"The girl – she could perhaps mend my socks and patch my shirts. Yours, too." Pop ran his hand through his thick hair and made it stand on end. "There's my advantages, son, but so far they have all been on their side. We don't know 'em, do we? They might be like Fred. Horrible thought! Have to wait and see." A glint came into his eyes. "I know what you're thinking about, Rob. Don't worry, I'm not a fool. Neither will I part with my money unless there's a good reason to make me do so. You know what they call me in town – Old Skinflint! I know." He nodded his head energetically. "What does the outside of Peppertree Lane remind you of?"

"An old barn," replied Rob promptly with another laugh. The old man was going to be sensible about this, thank heaven!

"Exactly. And what do I remind you of when I'm in my working clothes?"

"A hobo," said his foster-son candidly.

14

"And you look like an offshoot," answered the other. "We look as though we've no money, don't we? Nothing to spend on the house or ourselves. All we poor souls earn from the land goes back into it in machinery, seed, fertiliser – it has to, to make more money to buy more machinery to keep us occupied –"

Rob looked straight into the other's eyes and saw the determination and the humour in them and he sighed. "I see what you mean," he said softly.

"Glad you do." Another bunch of grapes was lifted from the brown earthenware bowl which was cool after being in the refrigerator all day. "I can't help thinking that if Fred lived well and spent all he earned his wife must have known all about it. Perhaps she helped him to get rid of it and did her share of spending too. We'll wait and see." This was a long speech from Pop. "That sort of thing is no good. You're all right, son, you'll never be poor, and I have more than sufficient for my needs. But Marie and her children get nothing from me unless they prove they're worthy of it. If they come good – well, then they'll be all right for the rest of their lives. If they don't –" He did not finish the sentence. "My nephew and niece – I don't like to refuse to have them. Do 'em good to have fifteen thousand acres to play in after living in a city."

"Just a minute." The other leaned over the table, pushing away the plates and the glasses so that he could rest his elbows on the stained cloth. "How old is the girl? She mightn't want to play."

"She'll be – ten years since I saw her. Ten and nine are nineteen – nineteen or twenty."

Rob whistled. "And what's she going to do when she's mended your socks and patched your shirts?"

A flicker of amusement shone in Pop's eyes. "Probably clean up in here."

"If she starts that I'm clearing out!"

"You can marry Valerie. Then you'll have to be tidy.

You can introduce Jean to Valerie. Nice girl." He nodded his head. "Pass on the word. We're paupers when the Delaneys arrive."

"As far as most folk in the Creek are concerned we're paupers anyway. So you've definitely made up your mind?"

"Definitely. It is the least I can do, Rob."

"If it has to be then I only hope you'll stick to what you've just said and go on being sensible about it." Rob looked at him under lowered brows. "They might not want to stay when they've seen it all."

"If they don't they'll be the losers in the long run," returned Pop confidently.

CHAPTER TWO

As letters were exchanged and plans made there were a few weeks' respite after that, for which Rob was thankful, as however much he thought it over he did not take kindly to the idea of three people coming from a city to share permanently the home he had with Pop, the only home he remembered. He fought against the idea as much as he dared, for the more he brooded over it the less he liked it all. Marie Delaney wrote many times, and it was obvious from her letters that she expected to come to a well-appointed home with all modern conveniences. Pop's thick brows drew together sometimes as he read the letters and his determination grew day by day and letter by letter that until he had seen his sister-in-law and her children and until they had lived with him for a while and proved their worth, he would not reveal the true state of his finances. She would never be without, he could not send her from his door empty-handed, but there was a difference between comfort and luxury.

In one letter she asked if it was necessary to pack all her household linen or could she dispose of that along with her furniture? Pop scratched his head over that question and went to look through untidy cupboards and drawers, scratching his head still more when he went through the dishevelled contents. Mrs. Delaney was told to bring all her linen and as much of her silver and crockery as she could, for he and Rob only bought what was necessary in that department. True, there were silver cups and rose bowls, won at various shows by his prize rams and ewes, but they had not been cleaned for many years and he felt almost ashamed of them as he moved them idly from one shelf to another in an effort to clean up.

The date of her arrival was definitely fixed, but then another letter came informing them that Nigel had spots; it could be measles, but she was not sure. "Fred would have known for certain!" was Rob's scoffing comment. So their departure was delayed a little longer. Finally Marie wrote again to say they were flying direct from Melbourne to Dubbo to save themselves the long train journey. She gave the date and time of their arrival and asked her brother-in-law to meet them with the car.

"And which of our many conveyances do you take to the airport?" asked Rob rather sarcastically when he had also read the letter.

"Certainly not yours," answered the elder man, thinking of the sleek convertible which had been his last birthday gift to his foster-son. "That shouts money."

A quizzical gleam came into Rob's eyes. "The bomb?" he suggested, and Pop hesitated.

"Think it'll get there and back?" he wanted to know. "It's almost dead. No springs, battery's flat, only three tyres –"

"Oh, Jack can fix that," Rob referred to the man employed in the machinery shed, who looked after everything mechanical on the station and who also attended to all the radio sets for everyone within a radius of miles. "It would help to create the right impression, wouldn't it?" he ended with a laugh.

In the cool of the evening, before leaving for Mudra Creek where he was attending a twenty-first birthday party, Rob looked over the old bomb, the name given to the car which had done good service over many many years but which was definitely ready for either retirement or the scrapyard. Many weeks had passed since it was last used and the interior was full of spider webs, dust, leaves, and dog hairs, for one of the numerous cattle dogs had made its bed upon the torn upholstery on the back seat. He wondered dubiously if it was safe to let Pop take this contraption to the airport; he poked round and sighed with relief; whatever the outward appearance, the engine was still capable of doing another few hundred miles and unless the back axle collapsed or the remaining three tyres blew out, he should arrive back at Peppertree Lane more or less whole. So thinking he wiped his hands on a piece of rag, told the mechanic to go ahead with the cleaning up and repairs and moved across to where his own car was parked beside a huge piece of farm machinery. The sight of it brought a contented smile; it had been wonderful to receive this on his birthday morning as a surprise gift, but it had been typical of the old man, the sort of thing he was always doing. Rob thought of the other expensive gifts he had received at one time or another, of the holidays he had had, and wondered how Pop Delaney would manage to curb all his generous instincts when his family arrived. He consoled himself with the thought that he knew also of the grim determination with which the old chap would and could carry out his ideas. If he was determined to wait six months or twelve to see how the newcomers settled to country life, he would do just that. Rob hated to think of anyone taking advantage of his foster-father.

"Thought you were going to meet Valerie?" asked a voice behind him. "Better get cracking, hadn't you? She hates to be kept waiting. Besides, it ain't polite! And you'd better make arrangements to leave that thing somewhere. Can't do with convertibles lying about, Rob."

"But it's mine!" protested Rob, turning to stare at him. "What am I to use when I go into town if I can't have this here?"

"Either the utility or this," said the other in the tone of voice which forbade any argument about it, and it was really only then, as he ran his fingers lovingly over the highly polished curve of the bonnet, that Rob realised just how serious Pop was about what he intended doing.

He was still thinking about it as he drove the old bomb

19

along the dusty road two days later, very much against his will. He had pointed out that he personally was not very interested in Mrs. Delaney and her son and daughter, he would meet them soon enough and have to put up with them in the house for a long time, but his arguments were all overruled and got him nowhere, and now he was behind the high wheel of the car with his foot pressed hard on the accelerator, trying to get some speed from the wheezy engine, and Pop was sitting beside him wearing his one good suit and with his hair neatly brushed and the white stubble removed from around his chin.

He was humming to himself as they moved along; the land on either side of the track was all his, and he was satisfied at what he saw. He turned his head to glance back at the homestead. From this distance it looked to be quite a pleasant place, being half hidden by the peppertrees. The red roof showed up in the sunlight, which also glinted on the huge water tanks at the side of the house, and he hoped that it would give their visitors a good impression when they saw it for the first time.

In his own way he had tried to make the interior look welcoming. Some of the many articles which had been lying about for days had been thrust out of sight and before he had left he had himself picked a large bunch of chrysanthemums from the untidy garden and placed them in the centre of the table in an earthenware bowl. He had also given strict instructions to Sam to have a meal ready upon their return.

In the small township of Murra Creek they stopped at the post office to collect the mail and were called into one of the numerous bars by some of their many friends in town for liquid refreshment before resuming their journey. Once on the tarred road they made better progress and Pop glanced at his heavy old-fashioned watch with satisfaction. The old bomb would get them to the airport before the plane arrived. He hoped he would remember Marie; it would be embarrassing if he greeted the wrong person. Jean would have grown beyond recognition and Nigel, the son, would be a perfect stranger.

The old car turned in from the road towards the airfield and came to a halt beside a new gleaming sedan. Rob edged in deliberately and pulled the hand-brake up with a vicious gesture. A few other people were standing about, some watching the sky, others busy talking and looking at an Auster nearby. Pop stepped down. Rob lit a cigarette and moved leisurely beside him.

"Nice position, this," remarked the older man, looking round with interest. "Good view, see for miles." He lifted his head. "Only just made it, boy. Here she comes!"

A black speck appeared from the south-west. As they lifted their heads to watch her approach they saw the undercarriage drop and the plane came round in a large wide sweep. Landing at the far end of the runway and with her engines roaring she came towards them, slackening speed as she drew nearer. Rob watched with a grin as his companion fumbled with his hat, touched the collar of his shirt, straightened his tie and shuffled his feet.

"Feeling nervous?" he asked solicitously.

Pop glanced at him. "I'm scared I might greet the wrong woman," he confessed, then he watched with interest as the huge plane came to a standstill and the motors died away. Men bustled forward with the moving gangway, the door was opened and a petite air hostess peeped out to see if everything was in order. One by one the passengers alighted, some casually as if landing from the skies was as natural as breathing or eating, others came down to Mother Earth gingerly, others thankfully. The two men looked at them keenly, then Pop smiled with relief.

"There's Marie!"

He might have known it, thought Rob. Marie Delaney would be the only one who had her arms full and who would stumble as she stepped on to the ground. Behind her

21

came a girl, but there was no small boy accompanying them.

"That must be Jean," murmured Pop, frowning a little. "But where's Nigel?"

He hurried forward and called, and as she heard her name Mrs. Delaney turned, met his gaze and gave a wan smile, then she hurried to meet him and immediately her handbag, two magazines and a small case fell to the ground.

"Oh, how silly of me! Hello, Gerald!" She took his outstretched hand. "Pick those up for me, Jean dear, please. How nice it is to see you again! It's been such a flight – air pockets or something, someone said – how are you?"

"I'm fine." Pop let go of her gloved hand and bent to pick up the case, for he thought his niece was overburdened as it was. "Jean? Welcome to the west, my dear." He looked at her keenly and smiled. "I thought you'd have grown more than this! But I should have known you. Where's your young brother?"

"Oh!" White-faced with alarm, Marie looked round. "Where's he got to? Hasn't he landed yet? Oh, Jean –"

"He'll be here, Mother," said Jean soothingly. "Don't worry. You know the pilot promised he could have a look into the control cabin. It's nice to see you, Uncle," she finished, avoiding her mother's reproachful glance. No, she was not going to kiss him; after all, the man was a stranger even if he was her uncle. She was not alarmed by Nigel's non-appearance, but looked round with interest, standing quietly with her skirt moving gently round her knees as the wind blew across the wide expanse of paddocks which bordered the drome.

Jean waited for her brother and noticed the young man standing nearby, returning his stare with hauteur. Immediately he grinned, and the colour rose in her cheeks as she pointedly turned her back on him and took the magazines

22

from her mother, tucking them under her arm and peering again at the aircraft.

As Pop talked to her mother Jean was aware of the young man taking the time to study her at his leisure. She wondered what he saw in her. A tiny girl who would barely reach his shoulder, she supposed, even with the high heels she was wearing. Her hair under her flowered sun-hat was probably her greatest claim to beauty, a rich brown and quite curly. At least she was conscious of looking her best today. There was a delicate air about her and her clothes were expensive, as were her mother's. Mrs. Delaney had insisted upon that. By dressing in their best for the first meeting with Pop they hoped to make a good impression.

Mrs. Delaney was beginning to get anxious about the non-appearance of her son and breaking off her conversation with Pop, turned to Jean with a worried expression. "Where's Nigel?" she cried in panic. "You told me, Jean, that he would be all right –"

"Here he comes now," Jean replied.

With one accord they all turned to look at the plane and a smile of delight spread over Pop's face as he watched a boy come from the cabin and stand on the top step.

He was wearing a spaceman's outfit and his head was enclosed in a plastic helmet, he had a ray gun in one hand and a torch in the other and there was a look of sheer devilment in his eyes, for he was full of the joys of life and had seen wonders never dreamed of before during the past few minutes. Behind him was the pilot, smiling widely.

Marie sighed. "I'm sorry, Gerald. He wanted to come like that, I said it wasn't the thing and that he should be properly dressed, but Jean took his part and between them my objections were overruled. I hope you'll be firm with him. Since Fred went he has tried me considerably, though I must admit he usually does as his sister tells him. I honestly don't know why I had a boy – girls are so much

23

better behaved and never let you down in public!"

"Hi!" cried the space man. "This is the Moon, isn't it?"

Pop shook his head as he hurried forward, the question had been addressed to him and he wanted a closer look at his nephew. "Not the Moon, son," he said gravely. "This is Venus."

Jean sighed as she watched the pilot follow the boy down the steps. Nigel turned to him and smiled, looking like a cherub through the plastic which covered him to the shoulders.

"Thanks for letting me look at everything. It was great! Gee, wait until I write and tell Brian all I've seen! He'll go green! Hullo, are you Uncle Gerald?" The helmet was removed and Nigel handed it to his mother, forgetting to be a space man as he studied his uncle for the first time. He looked candidly into the other's face and despite his mother's despairing cry of "Oh, Nigel, do remember your manners!" a cheeky grin spread slowly as he met the twinkle in the blue eyes. Gravely he shook hands, introduced the pilot and the air hostess. Pop watched Nigel take farewell of them, then turned quickly to the man who had been standing so patiently nearby.

"Sorry, son, I haven't introduced you. Marie, this is Rob Fraser – lives with me. And Jean, my niece." As Rob held out his hand and looked at her again, Jean flushed. This time there was no smile and she did not wonder, for she had rebuffed him with a look before. Why hadn't Uncle Gerald introduced him earlier? She had been very rude in turning so abruptly from his scrutiny, and what could be more natural if she was also going to live in the same house that he should want to see what she looked like? He himself did not look much different from any of the other men on the tarmac; like most of them he was wearing an open-necked shirt and grey flannels, a broad-brimmed hat was on his head and his face was tanned. He looked tall, but Jean had learnt from experience that because she lacked height others seemed to tower above her. His handclasp was firm and gave her the impression that he was very strong, then he turned from her and was laughing into the eager face of her brother.

"Our belongings are coming by rail," explained Marie as the small group moved away at last. "They'll be here in another week or so, I hope. How bright the sunlight is up her!"

As they neared the parked cars. Mrs. Delaney moved past the old bomb and turned to the new sedan, but Pop halted and opened the rear door, displaying to the world the torn upholstery and the tattered carpet which Jack had shaken and swept very energetically.

"This – this is your car?" asked Marie faintly.

"Gee, I thought it would be a posher one than this!" exclaimed Nigel, pointing his ray gun at it and pulling the trigger. "Jean said it was sure to be a big American –"

"Nigel, get in," commanded his sister.

Jean saw Pop exchange a knowing glance with Rob as he handed in an umbrella with the remark, "You won't need this much up here, Marie, unless you use it as a sunshade. Pass the case, Jean, I'll put it between your feet. Nigel, you sit in front with me.

Jean climbed in, sat down and gathered her skirt around her nylon-covered legs.

"I'm sat on a broken spring," announced a voice from the front seat.

"I'm sorry," apologised Rob seriously. "But the utility, the only other thing we have out at the station, beyond the tractors, of course, isn't as large or as comfortable as this. Wriggle about a bit, Nigel, you'll soon find a spot without a spring."

"Have we far to go?" asked Mrs. Delaney hopefully.

"Not far at all," Pop got in and slammed the front door hard to make it catch. "Forty miles."

"Oh! I thought it was nearer — aren't we in Dubbo now?"

"The town is two miles away. Don't go through there. We go the other way. All comfortable back there?" He turned his head to look at them. Jean sat upright, trying desperately hard to find a comfortable spot to perch, but failing and all too aware of broken springs. Her mother was still grasping her handbag and her umbrella. "All set, Rob. Let her go!"

As the car turned into the road the plane's engines roared to life again and it started taxing for the take-off. That kept Nigel on the one subject for quite a long time; he was telling his uncle and the other man — Jean could not make up her mind what his position was — all about the trip from Melbourne and how he had explored every inch of the plane and how he had been allowed to peep into the pilot's cabin and touch the controls. After they had landed, he added regretfully. Then he remarked that the plane was not as squeaky as the car and was far more comfortable. Jean exchanged an anxious glance with her mother and both of them stared at the back of the child's head, willing him to keep quiet and not repeat anything he might have heard when they had discussed this change so seriously; it had not always been possible to talk things over when he was either out of the house or asleep.

Jean knew Marie Delaney had not lied when she told her brother-in-law that Fred had left only debts. All her married life she had left monetary matters and business affairs in her husband's hands, chiefly because he always insisted that women could never understand such things, and so it had been a great shock when going through his private papers with her husband's solicitor after his death she had discovered there was nothing left. The rent of the house they were living in was high, situated as it was near one of the beaches on Port Phillip Bay, and she knew it would be impossible to go on living there. She had seen no other alternative but to write to Gerald. Jean was working in Melbourne, but she could not go on for ever as the sole breadwinner of the family.

Gerald was the only one who could help her in this crisis of her life, and the relief, when he had accepted her offer to take care of his home, had been great. Fred used to boast about Peppertree Lane, although to her knowledge he had never been there; he had told her of the size and beauty of the gardens, he had emphasised so many times that when his brother went the way of all flesh, his money would naturally come to him. It had been impressed upon her that Gerald was a man of consequence in Murra Creek and the surrounding district and that being on the land he had more money than was good for him. It had angered Fred that none of it had come his way during his lifetime.

Jean sighed, wondering, as she looked round at the countryside, if she had done the right thing in advising her mother to come. Nigel was the one she was most concerned about. He had a strength which amazed her, an exuberance which wearied her, an appetite which worried her and her housekeeping accounts and a tendency to accept all the peoples of the world as his friends, an attitude which had annoyed his father who liked to keep himself to himself. Surely the country life would suit the boy? He also needed the care and guidance of a man, didn't he? she asked herself miserably, still feeling slightly squeamish after her first flight, and looking out of the cracked window again. It was all so huge and empty, land stretched to the horizons without any of the houses or buildings to which she was accustomed. There were large paddocks, bare and brown after being newly ploughed, all the trees seemed to be of the same species and the air was hot and still. She glanced round the car and frowned. Anyone with plenty of ready cash would surely buy something better than this; it was most uncomfortable, and as she met her mother's eyes she grimaced slightly. She noticed immediately that the driver of the car had seen her do it. She met his glance in the driving mirror and saw the curl of his lips. She ignored him and turned her head to stare out of the window.

Nigel exhausted his chatter about the plane and began to take notice of where he was going. He remarked upon the size of the paddocks and the sameness of the trees, explaining that in Melbourne they had had the sea near at hand and pretty gardens and shrubs. Was there a lovely house at Peppertree Lane, he wanted to know, and wasn't that a funny name to give a house! She wondered what he was going to say when they came to the house for the first time. Would young Nigel blurt out that it was not all they had expected? That was very likely if his remark about the car was anything to go by.

"It seems a long way," cried the boy. "By now the plane must be halfway back to Melbourne!"

Pop smiled down at him. "Ever flown before?"

"No. None of us had. Mummy didn't want to come by train, having to go to Sydney first and then up here, she thought, I might get too tired and cross. I get awfully cross when I'm tired." He turned his head to smile at his mother and sister. "You're quiet — are you still feeling sick, Mummy?"

"I'm feeling much better, dear, thank you. But I shall be grateful to reach my journey's end and see this marvellous home of yours, Gerald. Fred used to tell me about it." As she leaned forward Pop gave a startled glance over his shoulder. "Have you many servants?"

"Good lord, no!" he exclaimed in surprise. "Only the men on the land."

"Oh!" she looked a bit taken aback. "Won't there be a meal ready when we arrive?"

"Sam should have everything well in hand," said Rob soothingly. "He's the station cook."

Servants! Jean pondered on this. Her mother seemed to have the impression from what Jean's father had told her of

28

his home that she was to issue orders to a team of maids. She saw the tightening of Rob's jaw and his sudden frown.

"Tell me about Peppertree Lane," Jean changed the subject adroitly. "It has such a charming and unusual name. Are there peppertrees, is that why it received its name?"

"Naturally," said Rob. "We aren't likely to call it The Laurels or The Cedars when there aren't any about! There are dozens of peppertrees, and as the house was built at the end of the original track which had the trees on either side, the name came naturally." He returned his attention to the road and Jean glared at the back of his head. All right, she thought, there's no need for you to be so snappish about it, I was only inquiring and keeping my mother and brother off what's evidently a delicate subject. "Nice house," he went on. "Large, airy rooms, very cool in summer."

Mrs. Delaney brightened a little and her conversation became easier. She talked brightly about the air trip from Melbourne and then looked ahead when Nigel pointed out the town ahead. Rob did not stop, but drove straight through, and they had only a glimpse of the shops and veranda-covered windows, of girls in light summer frocks and men in shorts and open-necked shirts.

"It doesn't seem a very large town," said Jean dubiously. "Perhaps that was only the fringe of it?"

"That was all of it," answered Rob, looking at her again in the mirror and causing her to bite her lips as she wondered just what his position was. He seemed to be very friendly with her uncle, more so than you would imagine one of his employees to be, unless, of course, the life they led out there among the animals made them appreciate each other's company all the more.

Unobtrusively Jean was loosening her coat and her mother had her shoes off, Nigel was obviously wishing he could take off his space-suit. The car slowed to pass over a ramp and the track became narrower. The three newcomers stared out of the windows, sensing they were nearing the house, for there was a line of peppers and Rob had turned the wheel of the car. With a squeak and a shudder she came to a stop and Pop opened his door.

"Welcome to Peppertree Lane," he announced. "We're here!"

Rather stiffly Marie stepped out on to the bare brown earth and looked ahead, her heart sinking as she took in the battered gate and untidy garden beyond it. Beside her Jean was staring at the vine-covered veranda, yet part of her was aware that Rob was watching their faces, which were very expressive. He had surely seen the flash of disappointment as they moved towards the gate and the hesitant way they walked up the path. On the veranda they paused almost unbelievingly. Despite Pop's efforts to tidy up the saddle was still on the floor. He had been going to move it when something else had claimed his attention and he had left it where it had lain for weeks. The cricket bat, now accompanied by a tennis racquet, was still there and the old cattle dog looked as though she had not moved for days. She did open her eyes and give a slight wag of her tail which moved some of the fronds of the fern, then she stretched and went to sleep again. They continued to hesitate, as though unable to believe this was Peppertree Lane.

"In here," Rob led the way into the dark hall which was bare of furniture and into the first of the large rooms which were dark and cool. Pop brought up the rear, carrying the two small cases they had brought with them, the umbrella and Nigel's space helmet.

Marie said nothing, but tears filled her eyes. She had come a very long way, venturing in a plane for the first time, she was weary and uncertain of herself, very hot, and could not believe this was true. Surely there was a mistake, for this was not what Fred had spoken about so often. The tears threatened to spill down her cheeks as she recollected that this was her home as she had no other, she had burnt all her boats behind her, and was very thankful for the comforting grip of Jean's hand upon her arm.

"Oh, Mummy!" breathed her daughter, but not so softly that Rob did not hear. Her mother gave her an agonised glance in reply as she moved from the room and walked as though in a trance further up the hall, peering into doors and finally coming to a halt in the kitchen. The linoleum was old and bare in patches, the huge fire oven seemed to glare at them defiantly across the room in the half light from the shuttered windows, there were shelves and cupboards which outwardly, like everything else, needed a coat of paint, and the two women shuddered to think of what they might find when they opened the doors. There was no sign of a meal or the preparations for one and Nigel frowned; he was very hungry and thirsty.

Looking round again before Rob led them to their bedrooms, he turned to his mother.

"There's no nice oven like you had," he remarked. "It isn't much, is it?" He suddenly felt very tired and cross. He had been fetched out of bed at a very early hour, the plane trip had tired him despite the novelty of it all, for he had had to sit still for four hours; he was hot and hungry and spun round angrily towards his sister. "You said it would be a lovely place," he cried accusingly before she could stop the flow of words. "You told me it would be nicer than the house we were living in. Well, it isn't. I don't think it's nice at all!"

CHAPTER THREE

JEAN, still flushed and feeling very annoyed by her brother's blunt remarks, turned on the tap and watched the brown water trickle slowly into the cracked wash basin. She bit her lips and then, very much against her will, the tears rolled down her face as she admitted to herself that Nigel was right. It wasn't nice. In Melbourne there had been a pale blue bathroom, with gleaming white bath and wash basin; there had been a shower recess and by turning the taps you could regulate the hot and cold water until it flowed at the temperature you wanted.

As yet she had not spoken to her mother, but she had heard her in the next room, rushing from one side to another in her usual flustered manner. Nigel was in a smaller room further away and kept running in, first to her and then to his mother, asking for the few of his belongings they had been able to bring by air. These consisted principally of guns and miniature cars, and she smiled as she thought of him.

He did not realise he had made a *faux-pas,* thought Jean forgivingly, as she watched the trickle of water. It had been a dreadful moment and she had felt sorry for both her mother and uncle, but what had annoyed her more than anything else had been the look on Rob Fraser's face. It had made her feel small and insignificant and gave her the feeling that she was of no consequence at all and that he was only putting up with her and her relations for the sake of the old man. He at least had given the impression of doing his best to make them feel at home; he had shown them their rooms and the bathroom, explained the heating of the chip heater for hot water for baths and had asked them if they had everything they needed. After the hot water service in the Victorian home this was of the most primitive.

And the trouble is, thought Jean, searching for the plug, we'll have to use it if we're to have baths!

There was no one about when she finally emerged from her bedroom feeling much fresher after a wash and change into clothing she thought very suitable for this, her first evening in her new home. Until the meal was ready she decided to explore the house and discovered the veranda ran round three sides. Most of it was creeper-covered, high and wide, and she realised how pleasant it would be sitting here in the shade during the heat of a summer afternoon. There was a lounge room with a wide open fireplace, which contained the ashes of the last fire burnt there and some orange peel, now withered and brown. There were only rugs on what had once been a polished floor, and experimentally she bent down and ran her hand over the boards; these were smooth under their coating of dust and if polished again would look rich and mellow. Glass doors opened from there into another large room which contained a full-size billiard table. Evidentally this was still used, for there were cues laid upon the green baize and the ashtrays were full of cigarette ends, some of which, she had noticed swiftly, were red with lipstick. So some women came here periodically to play billiards, and tentatively Jean picked up one of the balls and a cue and popped gently.

"Hm!" she murmured speculatively.

Glancing round with her finger to her lips she noticed the books which lined one wall. Their covers were tattered and upon investigation she found they were mostly on the subjects of breeding and rearing of sheep and the cultivation of the land. If she had lingered and read more of the titles she would have discovered many of Rob's old school books and others which had the name "Elizabeth Fraser" on the flyleaf.

More doors opened into the hall and Jean was surprised

33

at the number of rooms; it was a large house and had evidently been neglected, as many of the darkened rooms were without furniture. Unthinkingly she peeped into another room and saw the clothes tossed carelessly over a chair and the end of the bed and shut the door hurriedly, having no wish to be discovered by Rob looking into his bedroom. As she turned she made a mental note to dump all his belongings into that room at a later date. If she and her mother were going to do the housekeeping they would do it properly, and that meant Mr. Fraser could keep his junk all in the one place, she thought viciously.

Nigel was on the veranda having a feed of grapes and turned to grin at her as she joined him.

"Try some," he invited, pointed to a great bunch. "They're good."

Jean broke them off the vine and nodded her agreement as she tasted them.

"Uncle said he'd take us round and show us everything in the morning," her brother announced as soon as he could speak properly and before filling his mouth again. "Perhaps it won't be so bad here after all."

"I hope not." She looked round. "I wonder how Mummy is going to like it."

"She won't." Nigel shook his head positively. " 'Cos it's not as she said it would be."

"It will take some getting used to," admitted Jean. It certainly was not what they had expected and she looked at her mother sympathetically as Marie joined them. Gone was the navy blue ensemble and the flowery hat; in their place she wore an expensive nylon dress which flowed round her still slender figure.

"I had to put this on," she rushed into an explanation when she saw Jean looking at her magnificence with raised eyebrows. "I packed all the light things and thought we should be dining in state, as it were, our first night here. But – oh, Jean, it isn't at all what I expected it to be!"

34

Jean darted a warning glance towards her young brother and Mrs. Delaney nodded. "Yes, he's already opened his mouth too wide as it is!" she complained bitterly. "There was no need to say what you did, Nigel! With Uncle and that other man listening to you, whatever would they think! You forgot all I told you –"

"No, I remembered all you said," returned her son logically. "You told Jean that even being in the country wouldn't make any difference, you'd have all the gadgets you'd been used to, perhaps better ones. For you said Uncle was rich, Dad used to say so too!"

"I know he did." She spread out her hands helplessly and looked around. "If this is anything to go by, poor Gerald isn't rich at all. Oh, what are we going to do?"

"Have dinner," suggested Rob, coming down the hall.

"Oh!" she spun round. "It's so dark in there – we didn't hear you –"

Jean was trying to appear composed, at the same time she was wishing devoutly that he would not walk into their family circle at the precise moment as they were criticising Peppertree Lane and its contents. He must think them very rude.

"Do you live with Uncle Gerald?" she asked politely.

"I've lived with him for years."

"You work for him?"

"I work with him," he corrected. "Sam has brought the dinner over, so shall we go in? Pop won't be long, he had to see the men about a job he wants doing first thing in the morning."

In silence they followed him into the dining-room and Jean brightened a little when she saw that Sam had made an effort to make it appear cheerful. A large bowl of chrysanthemums had been placed on the sideboard and on the table were two small vases filled with red dahlias, the white cloth was fairly clean and so was the silver which, she noticed with an inward laugh, had all been placed wrongly.

"This looks pleasant," said Jean, smiling at the big man who did all the station cooking and who stood before her, looking like a giant, with a sheepish grin on his face and his huge hands moving nervously up and down his apron with which he had covered his grease-splashed trousers for the occasion. At least, she reflected, someone was trying to give them a welcome.

"A pleasure, miss," he assured her, and escaped as soon as he could to tell the others what the newcomers looked like.

"I rather like the look of him," said Jean to her mother. "He looks strong and dependable –"

"You keep away from the men," warned Rob. "Some of them are a bit wild, and none of us are used to having women about the place."

Her chin went up a little higher and she had to raise her head to look him in the eyes.

"You'll all have to *get* used to the idea," she retorted calmly, and he stared at her. She certainly didn't intend let this rude man intimidate her easily. She would give as good as she got! Perhaps working in a city had its advantages, it seemed to give the girls of today more of an independent attitude, and that was what was going to be needed here, she could see.

Rob grabbed the carving knife and attacked the large leg of mutton viciously, placing thick slices on each of the plates, afterwards adding piles of the inevitable pumpkin, potatoes and french beans. Marie looked at her plate in alarm.

"I shall never eat all that, Mr. Fraser!"

"Rob is the name," he answered casually. "And whatever else we may be short of out here it certainly isn't food. We grow it all, you see," he explained, looking at Jean. "We buy very little from the shops in town."

Pop came bustling in. He had discarded his best suit for the usual mode of dress in this part of the world and as a result looked far more at ease. He sat down and glanced round the table.

"Sam gone off his head?" he asked, pointing to the flowers, and Rob reminded him gently, "This is a special occasion, Pop."

"Don't usually have such fancy things," Pop explained to his guests, and smiled at Nigel. "That's right, boy, tuck in. Want to see you grow out here. Best place in the world. Plenty of sun, fresh air and good food. You'll soon lose your city pallor!"

Jean smiled. Marie, who rather treasured her delicate complexion, gave an inward shudder.

"I was just explaining that we grow all our own food," Rob looked round to see if everyone had all they required. "It's expensive getting it out from town."

"Too right," agreed Pop, and started on his dinner in earnest, commenting that Sam had improved his technique on this occasion.

Nigel was the only one who really did justice to what had been placed before him. Mrs. Delaney, after listening to her brother-in-law describe the marvellous fuel oven in the kitchen, found her appetite deserting her at the thought of it as she imagined standing there in the heat and the cobwebs cooking an enormous piece of mutton. Jean was regretting the grapes she had eaten; they had taken the edge off her appetite and she was so hot. As she pushed her plate away her uncle frowned.

"That won't do, girl. Must eat more than that. Not slimming, are you?" He darted the question at her and she shook her head.

"No, Uncle."

"Tired, I expect," he nodded his white head. "Fresh air. Not accustomed to it! Always does it to strangers – makes them sleepy."

The telephone bell rang in the hall and they all started. Rob excused himself and in the silence that followed his departure from the table they could hear his voice distinctly.

"Valerie? Why, yes, thanks. They arrived on time. You are? My dear, if you want me to take you you'll have to fetch me, because I won't drive that old bomb into town again today for you or anyone else! Sorry, but there it is." Jean listened while pretending not to do so, for his voice — he had a pleasant voice, she thought — had sharpened a little and he gave her the impression of being used to having his own way. "No, I won't drive the utility either," he said flatly. "Why not come out here and meet our visitors? Of course they won't mind!" He might have asked us before saying that, thought Jean. "You will? Good! See you later," he concluded casually.

The phone tinkled as he replaced the receiver and Pop raised his head as he returned to the dining-room.

"Valerie wanted me to make up a four at tennis, but I've suggested she comes out here instead." He glanced first at Jean and then at her mother. "She's a friend of ours –"

"Yours, Rob," murmured Pop into his glass.

"About my own age, I'm sure you'll like her." Jean noticed he refused to be drawn by Pop's interruption.

"I'm sure we shall," murmured Marie.

"I hope so," said Jean, returning the level glance.

"Are there plenty of young people in the district?" asked Jean, thinking she would not like to have to drive sixteen miles for a game of night tennis. Rob nodded as he watched Sam bring in a large steamed pudding. The two women flinched at the sight of it and then smiled slightly at the sight of the boy almost nodding over his plate.

Nigel went to bed quietly and without fuss or argument and the four adults sat on the veranda and talked spasmodically. Jean knew that Marie wished to speak to her brother-in-law, but not when Rob was there; she was uncertain as to his position in the household and had no desire to discuss her private affairs with one of Gerald's employ-

38

ees, however much he was in the old man's confidence. There was much she had to tell and much she wished to know about the future, that is if she could find the courage to ask. She had had visions of a settlement being suggested, but was feeling very doubtful about it now. She was not a mercenary woman, all her thoughts of any gain were solely for the benefit of her children.

She had wanted to make a good impression upon their arrival, but she felt all her efforts had been wasted on these two men. Feeling unhappy and uncertain over this change, she thought the difference between her old life and the new was going to take a great deal of getting used to and she would have to turn to her daughter for the courage and strength to carry on. Jean was a tower of strength to her mother. Marie had to rely on someone, for she could never trust her own judgment, and during the last weeks, Jean had taken control of everything in a businesslike, capable manner.

Pop had little to say either; he looked very thoughtful and was quite obvious of the many mosquitoes, moths and flying ants which fluttered round the bare electric light bulb and fell occasionally on to his bare arms.

Jean, half asleep, was sitting in one of the cane chairs, moving her hands quickly when mosquitoes, sensing fresh blood, alighted upon her. She wished this friend of Rob's was not coming to visit them, not on their first night here when she knew her mother wanted to talk to Uncle Gerald. Her eyes kept straying round the veranda, trying to picture this as her home. There was so much needed doing before it became comfortable – the sporting equipment would have to be put away in an orderly and proper manner, the dog would be banished and the saddle hung in the stable. That would be the beginning. When the dust was removed and some of the vines cut down she could visualise possibilities, providing of course that they were given permission to make such alterations, and she had a shrewd idea

39

that Rob would fight her to the bitter end as she suggested doing this and that. It was evident he resented their presence here, and she wondered why. What affair was it of his if Uncle's relatives came to live with him? She started wondering how many men there were employed on the property and how much land there was; a number of questions were hovering on her tongue, but she was becoming increasingly conscious of her drooping eyelids and the fact that Rob Fraser was alternatively watching her and watching the track, for headlights she presumed.

They came into view a few minutes later and he sauntered down the steps into the garden as the car swung round. It halted beside the gate which squeaked loudly as Rob opened it, a door slammed and a charming voice was heard to say in a bantering tone:

"Rob, if I didn't adore you so much I wouldn't trail out here because you were too tired to drive the old bomb in to meet me!"

Jean heard Rob laugh for the first time since they met and he came back up the path with the girl by his side, a lovely dark-haired girl wearing a thin cotton frock. Her arms were bare to the shoulder and beautifully tanned and her eyes sparkled as she stepped into the light of the veranda. Jean suddenly felt overdressed in her filmy nylon dress. This girl in the cheap cotton was smartness itself because of the way she wore it.

"Hullo, Pop." She smiled at him first, then brushed her hand gently over his hair in a familiar kind of way and turned to look at the visitors. Rob introduced them.

"Mrs. Delaney and her daughter, Jean. This is Valerie Miller."

Marie acknowledged the introduction with a smile, Valerie looked her up and down as she held out her hand.

"You make me feel so dowdy, Mrs. Delaney!" she cried with a soft laugh. "I appear in an old has-been and find you all dressed up for the occasion. Forgive me, please." She shook hands with Jean. "I'm very pleased to meet you and hope you'll like it here. But I'm sure you will."

"I'm sure I will too," returned Jean confidently. Miss Miller sounded as though she owned Peppertree Lane!

"You come from Melbourne? I have friends at Toorak and usually go down for the tennis tournaments. Do you play?"

"I do," Jean nodded cheerfully, thankful she had her racquets in the luggage coming by rail and quite confident in her ability to run this girl off any tennis court.

"That's nice." Valerie smiled. "You'll have to come into town and join us for a game some evening. We often have tennis parties at home; we have two courts, you know. I'll let you know when the next party comes along. It all depends on Mother — she has so many committees and so many visitors that we have difficulty in fitting everything in."

"It doesn't sound as though life will be dull out here," remarked Mrs. Delaney, sitting forward in her chair. "I'd been wondering what Jean would find to do with her time. She had a great many friends at home."

"Oh, she'll be able to go riding and play golf. When you get to know people you'll have invitations to all kinds of things," explained Valerie rather airily.

"Might have something out here," added Pop reflectively, and Jean shuddered at the thought of inviting people to a meal. Imagine Sam cooking for any friends she might make and serving them in that dark dining-room!

Rob looked at him. "Such as?"

"Barbecue. Plenty of sheep."

"That's about the only thing we have sufficient of," murmured his foster-son, and Valerie laughed at some hidden joke.

"What a wonderful idea!" She looked quite excited by the prospect. "It will have to be discussed again, Pop, thanks for putting the idea into my head. I shan't forget!

41

You know what I'm like, don't you? I never forget anything."

She stayed another hour, during which time she made it quite obvious that she regarded Rob as her own property. And she can have him with pleasure, thought Jean, who was sitting mutely in her chair wishing she could go to bed where she could puzzle out how she was going to ride, play golf and drive cars when no one had taught her to do any of those things. Marie made a tentative offer to make tea before the visitors' departure and was thankful when Valerie refused, for she remembered as she said the words that she did not know where anything was kept or if it was possible to boil a kettle or jug without having to light the fire in that terrible stove.

Pop continued to sit in his usual chair, listening to all that was said and just occasionally contributing a brief remark of his own, while Rob lay at ease in one of the cane chairs dangling a slipper from his foot and flicking matches or grape seeds out into the darkness. Valerie was obviously very much at home and when she finally did say goodnight and went out to her car, her conversation with Rob was carried on in a laughing undertone.

Jean rose, preparing to leave her mother alone to talk to her brother-in-law. But Marie motioned her to stay, obviously wanting her daughter's moral support for her conversation, and Jean subsided into a chair and remained in the background in case she was needed.

Her mother cleared her throat and made an attempt to still the agitated fluttering of her hands. Pop was a stranger, for she had only met him twice during her married life and the correspondence between the two brothers had been limited to one letter each year, usually at Christmas time. Yet there was so much to find out. What was to be the position of Jean and her mother at Peppertree Lane? There was the problem of Nigel – lessons would have to be arranged for him; the school was too far from the property to

42

go into town each day and Jean and her mother were determined not to send him away to a boarding school if it meant that their new relative was responsible for the fees.

There was silence. At last Pop said, "Tell me about Fred."

Mrs. Delaney was thankful he had made an opening to the conversation and told him quite frankly of the accident which had robbed her of her husband. The shock had worn off now and she could speak of it quite calmly. He listened, his gaze fixed on the dark garden seen only dimly by the light of the stars. Occasionally he nodded, then he asked point-blank how much money they possessed and Mrs. Delaney hesitated, then whispered of the small amount which had been transferred to the bank in Murra Creek.

"He must have lived well," Pop remarked, "for he had a good position."

"We had to have the best," she answered with dignity. "Fred had a position to live up to. But I must admit I didn't expect to find there was so little left, he never discussed financial matters with me." She bit her lip. "That was why I wrote to you, Gerald. I had – had to think of the children's welfare and of their future."

"Quite."

He doesn't help much, Jean thought wearily, passing her hand over her forehead. Perhaps he can't. Pop turned in his chair to look at her mother.

"After all you've had, Marie, this must appear lowly in your eyes."

"Oh, Gerald! What a thing to say! Of course, living out in the bush – one can't expect it to be like a city, can one? I mean, the conveniences and such – but you have electric light –" her voice faded. That at least was something to be thankful for.

"Think you're going to like it?" Another abrupt question to Jean this time.

"Yes – yes," she swallowed. "I'm sure we shall, when

43

we've had time to get used to it."

"That shouldn't take long. We have a great deal here you won't find in a city," he said gently. "When you've lived here for a while you'll understand what I mean, especially when you see your boy get some colour in his cheeks and some fat on his bones! Gradually it will grow on you until it's part of your life, and there'll come a day when you leave a city behind without regret and say 'Thank God I'm going home to the West!'" He grinned behind his hand at Mrs. Delaney's look of disbelief. "Anyway, as I told you in my letter I'm happy to give you a home. You'll have a good solid roof over your heads and four sound walls around you. In return you can look after Rob and me —"

"Who is he, by the way?" Jean interrupted him.

"On the wages sheet he's listed as a jackaroo," he explained vaguely, and she nodded, not wishing to show her ignorance. "We'll have to arrange a small housekeeping allowance, for extras, but I'm warning you, it won't be much," he told Mrs. Delaney.

"Yes, Gerald, I understand," she answered valiantly. "Thank you. I'm sure we shall manage." Greatly daring, she added, "Fred must have been mistaken about many things. He told me a great deal about Peppertree Lane —"

"As he'd never been here he had no idea of conditions," said Pop abruptly. "He must have been romancing — bad habit of his!"

"Haven't things been too good on the land recently?"

"Nature's unpredictable," he said, staring solidly at the grapevine. "Droughts one year, floods another. Sheep develop diseases or the wool doesn't come up to standard. Wheat gets rust and the yield isn't high. Many things can happen on the land, Marie."

"So it seems."

"When we get a good season we naturally have to buy

new machinery and replace parts of others. Very expensive tractors and such."

"I'm sure they must be," she agreed, totally out of her depth and realising only that her castle of dreams had fallen about her ears.

"We'll all settle down in a week or so. It will be strange for a while – only to be expected when you've made such a big change."

Again she nodded. Then Pop went on to explain about schooling for Nigel and that she and Jean would, between them, have to give the boy his lessons. The thought was sufficient to send her off to bed to have nightmares.

In the morning she went over the whole conversation with her daughter as they sat together drinking the strong tea which Pop had goodnaturedly made for them before he went out of doors. He had said the fire was already lit and had told Sam not to be worried any more about the occupants of the homestead, Mrs. Delaney would in future cook the meals and would give him his orders. They would be back for breakfast at half past seven, he added. Mrs. Delaney had fled into Jean's room after discovering Nigel's room was empty and she murmured hopefully that in such novel surroundings he at least should be happy.

"Aren't you, dear?" asked Jean, sitting up in bed and hugging her knees.

"Honestly, I don't know after what Uncle said last night." She frowned, then spread out her hands helplessly. "What can we do, child? If we return to Melbourne we have no home to go to and living there is so expensive. Oh, I wish your father was here to advise me!"

"If Father was alive we shouldn't be here now," Jean pointed out, stirring the strong tea absently. "We'll have to stay and make the best of it. Uncle has been very kind and I feel sorry for him. It's not his fault we were misled about his financial position. Poor old soul, he must have lived in this house for years without anyone to look after him properly, and it's time he too had a change."

"But where do we start? What do we do?"

"We'll start in the kitchen." Jean looked intent and serious. "Then we'll go into all the other rooms, one by one. They could be made so beautiful, because they're large and spacious –"

"But how can we when I'm only to be allowed a small amount of money for housekeeping? Knowing Nigel's appetite and neither your uncle or Rob, who's the jackaroo, whatever that is, Gerald didn't explain – where was I? Oh, I was talking about meals, I think. Never mind. What I meant was that you can't improve a house of this size without money –"

"Oh, yes, we can," said her daughter softly and soothingly. "You leave everything to me –"

"I'll be glad to," murmured Marie.

"We'll clean the whole place through for a start –"

"Perhaps they won't like that," said her mother doubtfully.

"If we're supposed to housekeep for them they'll have to like it! We'll polish every piece of wood in each room – that alone will make a difference, it's beautiful wood and there are some priceless pieces, especially in the lounge. But there are fingermarks and stains – yes." Jean looked at her mother's worried face thoughtfully. "We must do it, dear, for if we're to live here and entertain such visitors as the one we had last night we must have a nice home to welcome them to!" Marie nodded and Jean sat up straighter in her bed. "Do you know, that girl got under my skin a bit, she was too sure of herself! I'll show her a thing or two before I've finished!"

"You mustn't do anything to worry Uncle," began her mother hesitantly, then she looked again at her daughter's flushed face and cried hurriedly, "Oh, I know you'll behave yourself. I've wondered about her as well. She mentioned golf. You can't play."

"I can learn."

"And you can't drive a car either. Father always said it was too dangerous, and he didn't like women drivers."

"I'll learn to drive as well. All this land belongs to Uncle Gerald and if I can't find a few straight pieces somewhere to guide a car along, well, my name isn't Jean Delaney!"

Marie stood up and wrapped her white dressing-gown around her. "I wish I had your determination, dear. If you want to stay and make the best of it there's nothing more to be said. I only came for your sake and Nigel's." Her face became even more gloomy. "Gerald told me there was no school near to the township and that we shall have to give the child his lessons. They come by post from Sydney – oh, imagine trying to get some learning into his thick head!"

He isn't the only one who's going to learn, thought her daughter, watching as she left the room. There are one or two other people who are going to be taught something in the near future. I object to being surveyed and looked through as though I was incapable of breathing by that person who thinks he is a superior being! What I lack in size I'll make up for in impudence and other things!

CHAPTER FOUR

IT was Rob who showed them over the property later in the day. Jean was sure he only did so because he had been instructed by Pop to drive their visitors to each corner of Peppertree Lane and he promised fervently he would not forget. He brought the old utility round to the gate and waited until they had settled down on the uncomfortable seats, then, somewhat like a guide at a holiday resort, started off by showing them the men's quarters and the shed they used for packing fruit. He drove across a large paddock to the river bank, held out his hand towards it with a lordly gesture and said, "The Macquarie."

"Looks good." Nigel was the only person to speak.

The utility was backed away from the bank and he drove it to the first of the large paddocks which to Jean looked huge. The fence marking the boundary was minute in the distance and full of interest, she asked how large it was.

"A hundred acres," answered Rob briefly, and she whistled in rather an unladylike manner.

"Is this the largest paddock?"

"No. There's one of a hundred and fifty acres and another of a hundred and sixty. They're over the far side of that track." He pointed into the sunlight. "We'll be sowing wheat there shortly."

"What's that green stuff?" asked Nigel, pointing to yet another large expanse of land which seemed to stand out because of the brightness of colour in the bare surroundings.

"Lucerne."

"Oh!" All three Delaneys nodded. Nigel did not know what lucerne was and Jean had only a hazy idea that stock liked it as food and had no intention of showing her complete ignorance to this man who treated the whole outing as a boring necessity. They duly admired the cattle, fat, contented-looking beasts who gazed at them as they passed with soft brown eyes, and inspected some sheep. Rob went into technicalities about the shearing and pointed out the wool shed, he spoke of rams, ewes, wethers, Corriedales and Merinos and promised Nigel that later he could have a baby lamb all his own.

All of them were far too inexperienced to recognise the fitness of the flocks or the strength of the cattle. Rob told them woefully about stock losses, of fires which had rushed through these paddocks just before harvesting was due to commence and forgot to add that the last time it had happened was twenty years ago and he could not remember it himself. He painted a very dim picture of floods, causing Marie to glance up to the blueness of the sky and round towards the band of green which bordered the river bank, as if expecting torrents of water to fall from one and rush out towards her from the other.

Jean, listening carefully to all that was told her, stored it up for future reference and felt appallingly ignorant as Rob described something or other. Occasionally he became carried away in his enthusiasm and then the boredom would leave his voice and his face would change. Wonderingly she realised he loved it all; he was as much a part of Peppertree Lane as the very sheep. More than once he looked at her with scorn when she asked what she thought was a comparatively simple question. He certainly had more patience with Nigel, who, for once, appeared to be overawed by what he could see around him.

It was easy to understand the anxiety Uncle Gerald had at times and dimly the girl realised this was not an easy life; so much depended upon Nature. Her heart warmed towards him as she thought of the daily difficulties which attended his life – no wonder, if Rob was to be believed, and she saw no reason to disbelieve all he had told them,

49

the poor old man was finding it difficult to make ends meet. Her little jaw thrust itself higher into the air. She would do her best to help in every way she could to lighten his burden. For a start she and her mother would make the old homestead into a home worthy of that name, and afterwards – well, she would see if there were other ways in which she could help. She was convinced she was going to enjoy the freedom of these wild open spaces, which were more wide and more open than she had ever imagined they could be.

"How far is it from one boundary to another?" she asked Rob.

"Ten miles from the river bank to the far side of Jamieson's paddock," he answered promptly. "That's a name given to that part of the land because a chap named Jamieson shot himself out there."

Marie shuddered.

"Have you irrigation?" went on Jean, and he turned to look at her, apparently wondering at this sudden interest.

"Near the homestead and in the home orchard, but not out here."

"Why not?"

"It would be too expensive. There are water holes for the sheep and two or three bores, windmills – you can see one over there. They've never been known to go dry, so why bother about irrigation when the wind does the working of pumping water from the ground for nothing?" It was the tone of his voice more than the words which made Jean feel as though she had been put in her place, and she returned his glance with a level one of her own.

His hat was pulled well down over his forehead and hid most of his hair and his eyebrows were puckered in a frown as he watched one of the tractors in the distance, and again she wondered about him. Sam called him Mr. Rob and took due note of all that was said in quite a respectful manner; at breakfast time she had heard her uncle ask his

50

opinion about some matter of urgency which had cropped up and she had heard the note of affection in the younger man's voice as he answered.

The last place they drove to at the end of the morning was an orange orchard and Nigel gaped in amazement at the ripening fruit. The trees were all large and the oranges, mostly a pale yellow although many were still very green, hung from nearly every branch. Interspersed were lemon trees bearing both flowers and fruit at the same time and bees moved over them making the air sound lazy with their humming.

"Can I have one, please?" Nigel was down on the ground, peering at the nearest tree with great interest and with his hand outstretched in readiness.

"You can, but you'll probably have stomach-ache if you eat them now. They aren't ripe enough yet. Another few weeks and you'll be able to eat all you want."

The boy turned to Jean. "We'll still be here when they're ripe, won't we?" he asked hopefully.

"Of course!" She looked startled. "Whatever made you ask?"

"You didn't sound too happy about it last night. I want to, I like it even if Uncle hasn't any money—"

"Oh, Nigel!" she cried despairingly. "I *do* wish you wouldn't say such things!" Her face flushed uncomfortably as she felt rather than saw Rob staring at her. "We *are* going to live with Uncle Gerald. Don't you understand? We're staying here for ever."

"For ever is a long time," remarked Rob, kicking at the nearest wheel of the utility with the toe of his boot.

"And does the thought worry you?" asked Jean tartly, and his glance moved from the wheel and rested coolly on her face.

"Why should it worry me?"

"You sounded – annoyed."

"Did I?"

51

She looked him up and down angrily, unaware of her mother and brother staring at her in surprise.

"I don't see that it concerns you, anyway," she cried heatedly. "You're only an employee out here!"

Rob's face flushed a deep red, he opened his mouth, then closed it again. Let her think that if she liked; he could not care less. He slid into the driving seat and having no desire to be left out here in the middle of the property, Jean had no idea from which direction they had come or where the homestead was, so she took her seat in dignified silence and the utility bounded forward again along the track. Nigel was beside the driver watching everything with satisfaction and pleasure, deciding that as far as he was concerned they had done the right thing in coming to Peppertree Lane.

The boy ran wild during the following days, as they waited for the lessons and the timetables to arrive from the correspondence school in Sydney. His mother and sister were always busy and had little time to be bothered with him. As Uncle Gerald had assured them he could come to little harm and was not likely to get lost, they let him go and were thankful they had some peace for once. Nigel was only too glad to escape, he was beginning to love the old man with the white hair and the odd way of speaking; he possessed a strength of character which had been lacking in his own father. Not that the boy explained it that way, he only knew his uncle was prepared to explain matters and to show him things with great patience. His endless chatter was a source of great amusement to the two men with whom he spent most of his time. Occasionally he made some revealing remark and then they would exchange glances and Rob would nod as though to say, "I told you so!"

Jean was very busy. It was she who plotted and planned, and her mother fell in with all her suggestions and ideas for making the house more of a home with the least amount of expense. As it was the room where they both had to spend a great deal of their time and where there was least interference, they started in the kitchen. The tattered and faded Venetian blinds were ruthlessly torn down from above all the windows and Marie cried despairingly that the more light there was let into the place the more grime showed up. The ceilings and walls were brushed and then washed down, the cupboards were cleaned and they polished the old stove until it shone and discovered that beneath the layer of soot and dirt the old kettle was a bright shining copper. After that Marie did not hold such a grudge against the oven, which was a very good one for baking in, and her sponge cakes were fluffier and lighter than they had ever been before. This encouraged her to other things and Jean left her with the cooking, thankful that she was making the best of things and quite confident that with a little gentle prodding when she said she was tired and with a few suggestions here and there her mother would rise above the occasion and show Uncle Gerald and Rob, particularly Rob, that she was quite capable of doing all that was necessary without either grumbling or passing out under the strain.

Things began to look a little different in the house and it pleased Jean to see that Rob had noticed the changes. The smell of disinfectant lingered after the floors had been scrubbed, the kitchen seemed to alter its appearance looking clean and bright, she was sure, for the first time that he could remember. Sometimes when he went into the bathroom there would be a faint lingering perfume and Jean would notice his scowl. Gone were all the masculine bits and pieces he was accustomed to, his shaving tackle was neatly put away in a cupboard which was lined with clean white paper, fresh clean towels made their appearance with great regularity and the chipped washbasin was scrubbed each morning. The sun shone more brightly through clean windows showing up the battered plaster on the walls.

The veranda was cleared of all the bits and pieces which had lain about for so long. All Rob's belongings were

53

placed in his room, neatly left in a pile on the floor for him to sort out and put away. His was the one room which Jean refused to touch, and as it dawned upon Rob that she was doing it on purpose she became aware of his intense annoyance.

During the third week of their sojourn at Peppertree Lane Nigel started his lessons. These were held at regular times in a small room leading from the veranda where he could see nothing of what was happening and where nothing could distract his attention. He played up during the first two or three days and tired his mother, so much so that after he had been sent to bed in disgrace she sought out her brother-in-law and, because she was weary and annoyed she forgot her inward fear of him and *demanded* that he explained the situation to his nephew and withheld all further treats until he did as he was told and obeyed her during the lesson periods. Pop listened with a twinkle in his eyes. What transpired she never knew, but she found a better behaved boy waiting for her the following morning and had little further trouble with him. But always, as soon as the lessons were finished for the day, Nigel would vanish from her sight until the next meal time.

The telephone rang during one of those mornings and Jean went into the hall, wiping her hands on her apron and straightening her weary back. There was no mistaking Valerie's voice when she picked up the receiver.

"Jean? I hope you don't mind me calling you that, but it's more friendly, isn't it?" she began cheerfully. "I rang to ask if you'd like to come to dinner tomorrow evening? Mother is having one of her small parties and we thought it would be a good opportunity for you to meet people."

"That's very good of both you and your mother," answered Jean gratefully. "I'd love to come." There was eagerness in her voice.

"Not only you, dear. But your mother and brother as well —"

"Thank you. But Nigel goes to bed early," explained Jean hurriedly. She knew her young brother and his hearty dislike of afternoon teas and visitors. "I don't think parties are in his line at all! Not unless there are other children —"

"Oh, *no!*" Valerie sounded to be scandalised at the thought of having more than one child at any party of her mother's.

"Thank you for asking him anyway. I know Mother would enjoy it."

"I'm so glad. Rob will give you the directions as to how to get here, it's quite easy to find as we live on the outskirts of the town and you pass the end of the road as you drive in. About six? Would that suit you?"

"Thank you," Jean said again, swallowing hard, staring at the telephone which hung on the wall. How could she confess to this girl that she could not drive; in any case even if she could, would Uncle allow her to take the old bomb into town? It did not look safe, and she imagined you had to know its habits well to be able to drive it at all.

"See you tomorrow." Valerie rang off and slowly Jean replaced the receiver.

There was nothing else for it, she would have to ask Rob to take her into town. Otherwise both her mother and herself would have to forgo the chance of meeting new friends, and as they were going to live in the district for a long time the sooner the opportunity arose for meeting the people in it the better.

"Who was that, dear?" Her mother came out of what was now referred to as the schoolroom and shut the door quietly behind her. Nigel was very busy with a composition and as he was writing about what he had seen on the property it was keeping him quiet for a long time.

"Valerie. The girl who came here on our first evening. You remember her?" Jean moved slowly into the lounge where she was polishing the sideboard which almost covered the length of one wall. "She's invited us to a dinner party tomorrow evening. There'll be a few other people there too."

"How nice!" Marie's face changed and became lively. She had been used to a social life and was already missing her old friends and the gossipy little afternoon teas they had enjoyed in each other's homes. "We shall enjoy it, won't we?"

"No," said Jean hollowly, "we shan't. Not when I tell you that I'm expected to drive in, presumably in that old car —"

"You've never touched a car in your life!"

Her daughter bit her lip as she watched the animation die away on her mother's face.

"I'll ask Uncle Gerald or Rob to drive us in," she suggested.

"Are they invited to dinner too?"

"There was no mention of them."

"Well, how can we expect them to drive us and then to sit outside and wait until we're ready to return?" asked Marie slowly. "That would be a very bad-mannered thing to do. Oh dear, what a pity! I should have liked it, I know."

Jean put down the polishing cloth and ran her fingers over the end of the sideboard. It gleamed, something it had not done for years, and by the time she had rubbed over the whole surface she would defy anyone to say it was the same piece of furniture. It might be better if she stayed at home the following evening and went on polishing everything in the house. Rather that than having to ring up Valerie again and confess that she could not accept the invitation after all because she could not drive the car. She looked again at her mother's face.

"I'll find Rob and ask him," she said in a bright voice.

"He doesn't like us," cried Marie. "I've felt it since the

first day we were here."

"I shouldn't let the thought worry you," returned her daughter. "After all, he's only the jackaroo. *We* belong here more than he does!"

She hurried from the house into the sunlight wondering where Rob would be and what would be his reaction when she asked this favour. All was quiet and she walked through the gate, pausing as it squeaked protestingly behind her. A drop of oil would quieten that down and without hesitation she turned left and walked down the track to the machinery shed.

A head was bent over a tractor, then a grimy face was raised quickly at her entrance and she smiled at the mechanic, explaining quickly what she needed.

"That's something I could have done before, but no one asked me to do it, Miss Delaney," he said with a grin, looking at her frankly. "I don't do nothing unless I'm asked or told. Mr. Rob, he gives the orders in here chiefly and gets mad if it isn't done just as he says." He walked to the end of the shed and picked up an oil can. Jean was looking round with interest, noting all the drums of petrol, oil and kerosene the many tools, all of which were bright and clean and well looked after, as were the heavy farm machines not in use. Her eyes widened as she noticed many tins of paint. Some were new and unopened and she felt her fingers itch with the desire to find a paintbrush and do something inside the house. This was evidently where all the money went; it was obvious that nothing was spared to keep the tractors in working order and she sighed; a few pounds less in here and a few pounds more in the house – what a difference it would make to everything! With a last look at the paint tins she returned with the mechanic, who confided that his name was Jack and gave her leave to use it. He oiled the gate, swung it backwards and forwards a few times and they both nodded their satisfaction as the squeak vanished.

57

"It could do with a dab of paint too," said Jack, eyeing it with his head on one side.

"I was thinking the same thing," confessed the girl. "But we'll see about that later. I'm too busy inside to bother with this at present. Do you happen to know where Rob went to?"

"Mr. Rob? He went out in the utility, but where I've no idea. He doesn't tell me much." Jack smiled at her again and an idea began to form in her mind. He was a mechanic, he could drive everything there was at Peppertree Lane and would be the obvious person to help her. Impulsively she made her request, and he looked startled.

"If the Boss or Mr. Rob say it's O.K., Miss Delaney, then of course I'll teach you. You ask him."

"Thanks, I will."

In the meantime she had to find Rob, and wondered why she felt so shy and awkward about making her request. Perhaps because of the fact that since her arrival he had shown nothing but annoyance. There were times when the tone of his voice was — how could she explain it? Contemptuous. That was the only word to describe it, and Jean frowned. What had she done to be treated in such a manner by a mere jackaroo?

Nigel and Rob appeared an hour later. They walked together towards the gate and on the veranda Jean waited for them, a smile flitting over her face as she listened to her brother's voice. It went on and on, in fact it started as soon as he opened his eyes in the morning and died away only as he drifted off to sleep. He bounced first through the gate and shouted a greeting when he saw her. Rob followed more slowly and halfway up the path he stopped and frowned. Something was different. He looked round, nodded curtly to Jean, then turned his head and peered back along the track.

"What's the matter?" asked Nigel curiously.

"Something is not as it was."

The boy walked to the gate and hung on it as he looked hopefully up and down.

"It's the gate," he announced, and slammed it hard. "It doesn't squeak any more."

"But it's *always* squeaked," cried Rob.

Jean stepped down from the veranda. "I asked Jack to oil it," she explained. "It had squeaked long enough."

"I'm glad you thought so," came the retort.

"It also needs a coat of paint." She surveyed the stained and cracked wood with her head on one side. "One of these days, when I have time, I'll do it. I'm sure I shall like painting."

"There's no money, for such things —"

"No money needed," she answered, smiling up at him. "I noticed there were a great many tins of paint in the machinery shed, and some were opened. I could use those." She returned his frowning stare with a puckish grin. "I'll ask Uncle," she added wickedly, knowing that Rob could say no more. This small request would be granted by Pop without hesitation.

Jean smoothed down the apron she was wearing over a light frock, realising for the first time that she had not worn a coat of any description since coming here, and raised her eyes to meet his angry ones.

"I'm sorry if oiling the gate has put you in a temper," she said. "Because I was going to ask you a favour."

"Were you?"

"It's no use if you're still annoyed, so it doesn't matter." She slipped her arm round her brother's shoulders and moved back towards the house, adding over her shoulder, "I'll ask Uncle."

She saw Rob scowl, turn back quickly through the gate and walk towards the machinery shed.

Half an hour later, as Jean was putting the finishing

touches to the dining-table and her mother was in the kitchen making gravy, a burst of music made them both raise their heads. The old piano in the lounge was being banged viciously but tunefully and Pop, coming up the garden path, laughed softly as he entered the house.

CHAPTER FIVE

THE dining room both looked and felt different, and Sam had never laid a table in such a manner; the silver was polished and correctly placed, the white lacy cloth, one from Marie's collection of household goods, was clean and shiny. The men of the household knew nothing about starch; they had always been content to boil everything but their socks in the large copper in the laundry and run the iron over them when there was time or when they felt like it. Now things were different, Jean reflected as she came into the room carrying a covered dish. The sideboard, a smaller one than the one in the lounge, looked a different piece of furniture altogether. It was a piece which had been brought out from England by Pop's grandfather or great-grandfather, she forgot which he had told her, and it had been old then. The old wood had responded nobly to the polishing it had received.

Pop was bending over the silver rosebowl that Jean had found at the back of a cupboard in one of her foraging attempts.

"I found that – I hope you don't mind, Uncle," she said hastily, "but to my mind it was too lovely a thing to hide away, so I rubbed it up."

"It's all right, girl." He sniffed with appreciation and forgot the rose bowl. "That smells good!"

"It is good. And it's surprising what can be done with mutton. Don't you ever have beef, Uncle? That would be a change."

"In the winter, girl. Too much meat on a bullock to have it hanging about for any length of time."

She thought of sides of beef hanging in the kitchen, with

61

her mother slicing off pieces as she needed them and nodded her head. The heat would beat them to it within a couple of days and the fridge would be totally useless as it was rather small and they were having difficulty in finding room in it now. There was butter, freshly made each two or three days, fresh cream every morning, more milk than they knew what to do with despite all Nigel had, and the half sheep which one of the men brought up to the house twice a week. Even her mother admitted there was food in plenty and she had ordered little from town, consequently the money she received from her brother-in-law was not spent and she had confided to Jean that if she went very carefully and saved for a month or two it might be possible to do something about the atrocious curtains in the various rooms.

Rob came in and sat down in his usual place. Jean looked at him with her head on one side.

"Are you still annoyed about the gate?" she asked with interest, and when he did not reply she turned to her uncle. "Would you mind if I painted it one day? It needs it badly and I discovered some tins in the machinery shed –"

"Those are for the tractors and various other things," interrupted Rob. "I bought each tin with some purpose in mind."

"The gate would need very little. I'd rub it down with sandpaper first, then give it some undercoat. I noticed a tin of that as well. It would improve the look of things outside."

"Then there would be the fence," snapped Rob. "And the front door –"

"Yes, it would show up all the other faults, wouldn't it?" she admitted. "I don't mind doing them all in time. May I, Uncle, please?"

"Yes," he nodded, laughing.

"You're a dear," she smiled at him, and bent to inspect Nigel's hands, giving her approval when she saw that they were clean. "There was something else I wanted to ask as well – I did intend asking Rob, but he was annoyed with me, so I didn't. Valerie rang up this afternoon," Rob raised his head quickly. "She asked Mother and me to dinner tomorrow evening and must have thought I could drive. Well, I can't, but I'd like to learn as soon as possible – that is, of course, if you'll give your permission. So would you mind taking us into town, Uncle, please? She wants to introduce us to some people and it would be nice to know everyone."

"Is the boy invited?" he wanted to know.

"Yes. But I thought visiting wouldn't be in his line and refused on his behalf."

Nigel nodded. He had no desire at all to visit with his mother and sister, for it would mean he would have to be on his best behaviour for hours on end, and could anything be more tiring? He much preferred to stay here and assist the men in whatever they were doing, especially as the daylight faded so quickly and it was dark about half-past six, it did not give him much time when lessons were finished. Yesterday he had been with Jack on one of the tractors, he had accompanied Bill to a paddock many miles from the homestead and Rob had taken him to the river and had pointed out the safe places for bathing, the depth and the many snags, mostly fallen logs and trees.

"I'd rather stay here," he said firmly.

"But if I go with Jean who's to put you to bed?" asked his mother.

"The boy can undress himself, can't he?" asked Pop.

"Of course I can!" Nigel was very indignant. "I'm ten!"

"A terrific age," agreed his uncle. "All right. Rob will take you into town, girl. Shall be busy myself, but I'll keep an ear open for Nigel. In case he cries in his sleep, eh?"

The child opened his mouth to deny the fact that he was a baby and ever did such a thing, then he saw the old man smiling at him and he smiled back understandingly. It would be a bit of fun to have Uncle there at bedtime, perhaps there would be a story about bushrangers or blackfellows; if not it would be a change not to have his mother fussing round for once.

"If you're sure –" began Marie hesitatingly, and stopped as her brother-in-law looked at her beneath his bushy eyebrows. "Oh, yes, Gerald, if you want to, of course, and if you don't think he'll misbehave –"

"Not with me he won't!"

"That arrangement doesn't look as though it suits everyone," murmured Jean, stealing a mischievous glance at the face of the man on the opposite side of the table.

"Rob will take you and your mother into town," repeated Pop calmly. "Valerie is his girl-friend anyway, he never lacked an excuse to go and see her before you came."

"But now perhaps he's afraid I shall start oiling and painting everything in sight on the property in his absence," retorted his niece very tartly.

Rob, behind the driving wheel of the old bomb, concentrated his whole attention on the road ahead. It was clear that he was dreading needless chatter and numerous questions which would need an answer, but Jean did not bother to speak, her whole attention being on whatever she could see from the car windows.

Jean was wearing a frock of jacaranda blue which was plain and neat, an ideal dress for both the evening and the occasion. Marie was in black which gave her a look of fragility; there were pearls round her throat and in her ears and for a moment Jean wondered what Valerie's mother would think of her guests. She had heard from Pop that Mrs. Miller was the unquestioned leader of fashion in Murra Creek, a position she had held for years, although of recent times her position had become a precarious one owing to the unconscious grace and beauty which a certain Mrs. Kennedy had brought into these functions.

Jean began to hum softly beneath her breath, not at all

perturbed at the thought of meeting a houseful of strangers.

"Will you teach me to drive, please?" she asked suddenly, and Rob replied before he had the chance to think it over:

"No!"

"How very definite," she answered quietly. "Never mind, I'll find someone else."

"Who else is there at Peppertree Lane?"

"Jack, the mechanic. I mentioned it to him yesterday."

The car swerved. "Surely you haven't been hobnobbing with the men?" he snapped, and she nodded.

"I speak to them – in fact, I like them all. They're not rude to me, and after all, I'm not a snob."

She knew he felt a great desire to shake her.

The rest of the journey was a silent one. Jean continued humming and wondered if her mother would ever come to like this part of the country. Everything was so very different from all she had ever been used to. To begin with, she missed her friends and neighbours; she found she was beginning to long for the cool grey days which were Melbourne's lot at times, and she missed the sight and the sound of the sea. The big unfurnished house depressed her; she wanted light cheerful things around and thought that if only everything had been different and Gerald really had made a fortune, even a small one, and she had been allowed to run riot with a cheque book in a large store, how much more home-like she could make Peppertree Lane. She was still afraid of Gerald, for he was not at all as his brother had been, he had a way of looking at her sometimes which made her feel uncomfortable, as though he was searching her face for signs of discontent or unhappiness she confided to Jean. Jean encouraged her when she was downhearted and reminded her that they were lucky; they had generously been given the free run of the house and the whole estate, they had good food and no bills, and Nigel, who was the darling of their hearts, had already remarked that it was a wizard of a place and he hoped he would never have to leave. There was so much for a chap to do, and when he grew up he was going to drive a tractor and give orders to the men. Marie smiled a little as she thought of her son and his many enthusiasms, and as Rob announced curtly that they were nearly there she sat up and began to touch her hair, patting it gently back into place.

The car slowed and turned into a short drive before coming to a halt outside a large brick house. Like most country homes this had verandas and in the bright lights, for it was now quite dark, she could see numerous people seated on brightly painted chairs, she could hear the clink of glasses and the talk and laughter.

"Rob!" There was a delighted call from Valerie as she recognised the driver of the car and leaving her guests she came running down the steps to meet him. "This is a surprise! When I asked you to come you refused because you wouldn't use the old bomb, and now you've turned up with the guests!"

"I'm afraid it was all my fault." Jean stepped from the car and smiled. "Uncle wouldn't let me use this old thing, you see. It looks as though it's liable to collapse at any moment, doesn't it?" She pretended not to see the look of incredulous indignation on Rob's face and she smiled again at Valerie – let him get out of that one, she thought. And I didn't lie either! "How are you? I've been looking forward to meeting you again."

"Sweet of you to say so," Valerie laughed. "Come in and meet my mother and the other folk."

"And what do I do?" asked Rob, lighting a cigarette. "Wait here until the ball is over?"

"You're a grumpy darling, aren't you?" Valerie put her hand on his arm and looked up into his face. "You know quite well that you're as welcome here as the rains when they come. Take that sour look off your face – acting as chauffeur should be a novel experience for you."

66

"It wouldn't be so bad if I had a decent car," he grumbled as he followed them up the steps.

"Why, what happened to the convertible?" asked a girl standing nearby, and Rob shot her a glance almost of dislike.

"Had to sell it to pay some bills." It sounded like a joke, and Mrs. Delaney and her daughter took it as such.

There followed a great many introductions. Jean smiled at everyone, said she liked the district although as yet she had not seen very much of it; yes, she was quite happy out at Peppertree Lane, and was very pleased to meet everyone. Mrs. Miller proved to be a graceful sophisticated woman, who spent most of her time in her other home on the outskirts of Sydney. She did not walk, she glided, and Jean watched with fascinated eyes as she moved across the veranda. Not a hair of her head was out of place, not a wrinkle showed on the smooth skin, and the girl wondered how much of her day was spent before her mirror attaining this perfection and if she ever stood over a hot stove cooking meals. The latter she doubted very much, for her hands were long and white and her nails a delicate pink. She glanced at her own mother and sighed with thankfulness as she met her eyes.

There were a great number of young people and all were friendly towards the new arrivals. Glasses were thrust into their hands and when Jean took the first sip she pulled a face, Rob, standing between her and Valerie, glanced down in surprise.

"What's wrong with it?" he wanted to know.

"Beer!" She gave Valerie a humorous glance. "I'm sorry, but I don't like it." And the glass was placed back on the tray she was holding.

"Oh! Perhaps you'd like lemonade. Or water?" There was a faint raising of delicate eyebrows.

"Thank you," said Jean gratefully. "Lemonade. That's much more in my line!"

67

Valerie turned, winked at a boy standing nearby and moved over towards the cocktail cabinet and a woman sitting near the door smiled at Jean in a friendly manner.

"That was very rude," said Rob, bending his head towards her. "You could have pretended to like it – everyone else is drinking it."

"Why should I pretend?" she wanted to know.

"Manners!" he hissed.

"I shouldn't have had any manners or any reputation left at all if I had drunk it," she answered candidly. "I think I should have been sick all over the floor."

Rob stared at her. One or two people were looking with amused interest at this young lady who stated her wishes so clearly. Jean was not conscious of having said anything out of the ordinary; she continued to look round, smiling when someone nodded to her. Valerie returned with the lemonade. "This is quite harmless," she smiled. "Personally I much prefer something with a kick in it."

"Ah, thank you." Jean took the glass gratefully. "I get enough kick out of life as it is," she added, and Valerie flushed suddenly.

Dinner was served in a delightful modern dining-room which faced on to the garden at the side of the house, and Jean, with an experienced and housewifely eye, noted everything for future reference. There would come a day when visitors would be invited to Peppertree Lane and she wanted to learn as much as she could about country visiting before that time came. It was so different from what it had been in Melbourne. There was less formality for a start, everyone called everyone else by their Christian names. The food was mostly cold, cunningly and beautifully garnished, and so it became even more appetising; it was nicely served and she could not find fault anywhere. Mrs. Miller had made her welcome and she was not feeling out of place. She glanced down the table to where her mother was sitting, thankful she had been able to come, although if this was a small dinner party, what would a large one be like?

Guests drifted back on to the verandas and Jean found herself sitting next to the woman in grey who had laughed so delightedly before dinner.

"Miss Delaney, may I applaud your discretion?" she began. "I dislike beer myself."

"Oh! Oh, do you? I'm so glad I'm not a wallflower." With unconcealed interest she looked into the other's face.

"You'll never be that," returned the other softly. "It's so refreshing, too, to meet someone who doesn't mind saying what she thinks! I like to do it myself and get plenty of candid comments at home! Forgive me if I sound personal, but I do admire your dress – it's a beautiful colour and it does suit you."

"I made it myself," said Jean simply, and the other's eyes widened in astonishment.

"I shouldn't tell Valerie that," she murmured. "You may go down in her estimation."

Jean looked at her searchingly, wondering if there was any hidden meaning, but the other's eyes met hers with only a hint of friendly laughter in them and the girl sighed. She felt she could trust this woman and hoped she would see more of her in the coming months, maybe years, when she would be at Peppertree Lane.

"I made Mother's dress, too. In fact I do a lot of sewing, for I worked for a very exclusive dressmaker in Melbourne."

"So that was it! There's been much speculation in Murra Creek about the new arrivals at Peppertree Lane. We're not a large community and anything different is of interest. Tell me about Pop and the house – it's a long time since I was out there to see him."

"Oh, you know him?" Jean looked pleased. "He is a
69

dear, but oh, he has to work so hard." She began to chatter excitedly, telling her new-found friend her impressions of the property which was now her home, and as she described all she and her mother had been doing her companion's eyes widened in surprise and something more than that.

"But you look such a slip of a thing!" she exclaimed.

"My looks belie me," said Jean seriously. "Candidly, I'm tired of people thinking I'm weak and helpless because I'm so small. Rob – do you know him too? He gives me the impression that he thinks I should still be in the schoolroom!" There was indignation in her voice and her companion laughed again.

At the other side of the room Valerie appeared to be enjoying herself chatting to a friend. In one of those sudden lulls in conversation which happen at all parties her words carried quite distinctly across the room.

"Mr. Delaney's niece," Jean heard her say. "Oh, no, I don't think she'll be staying out there –"

Jean raised her head.

"But I am staying at Peppertree Lane," she said clearly. "That's our home now."

The mask of polite interest slipped for a moment from Mrs. Miller's perfect face and Marie looked a little shocked at the way Jean had called attention to herself. But at that moment an abrupt voice was heard outside the veranda, requesting whoever had left a heap of rusty scrap-iron in the driveway to come and remove it immediately.

"That will be the old bomb he's referring to," said Rob, and moved quickly from the room.

"And that will be my husband," Jean's companion nodded. "He usually manages to announce his arrival with some such remark!"

"I don't know your name," the girl looked at her shyly. "I believe we were introduced, but there were so many – please forgive me."

"I'm Anne Kennedy. We live on another property along

70

the river bank – Gum Valley. Pop might have mentioned it to you. Do drive over and see me one afternoon, you'll be very welcome."

"Thank you. But as yet I can't drive. Oh, I've said that so many times recently and I'm getting tired of it." Her forehead creased. Everyone took it for granted that she could do all these things; evidently the country women were as much at home on the golf links, on horseback or in cars as they were in their own kitchens.

"Surely Rob will teach you –"

"Rob won't." Jean looked annoyed. "He said so, most emphatically, not so very long ago.

Mrs. Kennedy was watching and saw the determination in the set of the small jaw and nodded, smiling to herself.

"Teach yourself, Jean. It's not difficult. Take the old bomb out into the paddocks where you won't harm either it or anything else –"

"But the gears and things!"

"You have a young brother, I've heard. Take him with you, he'll know more about such things than you give him credit for."

Jean looked very thoughtful and did not raise her head when Rob and another man came into the room, the latter to be greeted gushingly by his hostess. He came towards them and Jean only murmured something trivial when he was introduced to her and he glanced at her with some surprise. Mrs. Kennedy waved him away.

"I'll see you later," she whispered. "At the moment we're very busy concentrating!"

Obediently her husband turned, with one eyebrow raised, wondering what the conversation was about. Jean was unconscious of being rude, she was thinking of Nigel and the old bomb, of placid horses who would not mind if she mounted them and walked them slowly round the paddocks, and of practising shots across logs and anthills as she learnt to handle golf clubs. It was all going to be very

71

difficult without a coach or a teacher, but she would do it somehow. Her jaw jutted out still further. If Valerie could do these things, so could she! But – there was a large but. She had no clothes suitable for riding, no money to spare for such things as niblicks – she knew of no other iron used in golf. But one thing at a time, she told herself sternly. Cars first. The intricacies of the old bomb would be her first task, then, when she felt confident and had managed to pass her driving test, she would turn her thoughts in other directions. Perhaps she would be able to drive to the golf course and watch the players from some hidden spot. Riding should not present many difficulties. It looked easy – you sat on the horse's back, tugged at the reins and it moved forward with you sitting upright.

"Simple!" she murmured.

Discussions were in progress in various parts of the rooms and on the verandas, about the lack of follow-up rains which would ensure the winter feed, the condition of sheep and, by those who had attended, the merits of the Royal Easter Show in Sydney. The latest engagement was discussed at length, then someone announced that someone else had had a baby and so the topics changed. As she listened Jean laughed inwardly at the amount of ground covered in such a short time. It was the same no matter where you went, or who you were with, a subject was brought up, discussed or argued about, and then an odd remark led to a different idea altogether; a woman was now describing a journey she had paid to the Great Barrier Reef and that reminded Mrs. Miller of a visit she had made a year or so ago to the Islands, and within a few moments everyone recollected some strange or humorous incident which had happened on their travels.

Her mother was enjoying herself. She had met someone about the same age as herself who also had a son and daughter and they exchanged confidences, sitting in comfortable chairs and with ice-cold drinks always before them on a small table. Mrs. Miller spent most of her time with her own friends, always gracious and smiling, looking as cool and serene at the end of the evening as she had done at the beginning. Valerie was everywhere and was very popular, but there was smouldering anger in her eyes whenever she looked in Rob's direction. He sat by an open window, staring into the night at the silhouette of the old car parked on a grass verge nearby, fanning his anger, until Valerie told him to snap out of it and come to the piano.

Many people seconded this request and he allowed himself to be led across the room, Valerie's hand through his arm. Once there in front of the piano he forgot his ill-humour and set out to entertain, soon young voices were raised in accompaniment, then the old people joined in with requests of their own and the evening finished on a highly successful note.

Valerie walked to the car when Jean and her mother left, shut the doors after they had taken their seats and turned to Rob.

"I'll see you at the weekend as we arranged previously?" she asked, and he nodded. "If you would rather I'll come out for you in my car and you could stay the night here. As we're playing tennis on Sunday it would save you trailing back again."

"Suits me," he agreed, and Jean thought that it was no unusual occurrence.

Valerie smiled in the darkness. "I'll arrange a game for you some time next week, Jean."

"That's very kind of you."

"Did you play competition tennis or were they just friendly games?"

"The former," said Jean rather shortly.

"Oh! I just wanted an idea of your game – if you're used to hard tennis it's no use asking rabbits to play with us, is it? I don't suppose you've ever won any cups?"

"Only eight," answered Jean sweetly. And that will give

73

her something to chew on! she thought, using some of her brother's slang. If she doesn't believe me, or if Rob accuses me of lying, as he may do, saying I'm not big enough to hold a tennis racquet, I'll arrange all eight cups on the mantelpiece in the lounge.

She was glad Rob would be out of the way for a couple of days; it would give her a chance to put into effect some of her plans without having him glower at her, and as they drove into the night she wondered what would happen if he returned home and found the gate painted a nice bright green.

CHAPTER SIX

JEAN was silent on the drive home. All her attention was focused on what Rob was doing with his hands and feet; she watched every little move he made and remembered it all. Never again would she ask Rob to teach her anything, she would learn it all herself and then show him she was quite capable of doing these things he did automatically. Pressing imaginary brakes with her foot as they slowed for a ramp, she felt pleased with herself and blessed Mrs. Kennedy for putting the idea into her head.

"Who is Mrs. Kennedy?" she wanted to know suddenly, breaking the silence for the first time.

"Mr. Kennedy's wife."

"I really didn't think she was his mother," she retorted. "Are you still annoyed about the gate?"

"Yes."

"What a baby you are!" she murmured almost indulgently, and was surprised at the sudden burst of energy which seemed to spring from the old bomb. Rob had his foot pressed hard to the floor and the ancient engine responded to his mood as best it could.

As they reached the last ramp before turning into the property, she cried, "Stop!" in such a tone of voice that Marie, who was half asleep, sat bolt upright in her corner and Rob instinctively jammed on the brake. The car came to an abrupt halt and Jean was out of the door in a flash, Rob following nearly as quickly, wondering if she had been taken ill or if she had seen something or somebody on the track.

"Have you a light?" she called from the rear of the car and in the dull red glow of the one tail lamp he could see her bending over the iron grid which formed the ramp, her dress trailing in the dust.

"Only matches. What's the matter? What have you seen?"

"There's a dog here, I thought I caught a glimpse of it in the headlights. Then I heard it whimper as we passed near; it must have been here earlier in the evening and we didn't know."

"Oh, is that all?"

"What do you mean, is that all?" she flashed in reply. "Bring a light, strike a match, do something – and stop being so boorish!"

"Jean! Jean!" admonished her mother gently behind her. "That's not the way to speak, child."

"I don't care." There was a sob in the girl's voice as she bent lower. "It's injured, it can't move – yet he asks is that all!"

Scorning his hesitant offer of assistance, for Rob had been surprised at the vehemence in her voice, Jean scrambled down beside the animal and drew in her breath. In the uncertain light she could see the dog lying on its side, its tongue hanging out, panting with thirst and exhaustion and she put her hand out gently to touch him.

"Mind he doesn't bite!" called Rob sharply, who knew the uncertain tempers possessed by the cattle dogs.

"He won't." She sounded confident, but he moved down beside her ready to grab the dog by the scruff of the neck if it showed any sign of snapping.

In the twelve months of the dog's existence his meals had consisted of lumps of raw meat flung into the dust and he had had to fight to get his share. His ears and nose bore the scars of those skirmishes. He had padded for miles along stock routes in the heat, at night he had stretched out in the comparative coolness of the dark trees, in the wind and the rain he had trudged behind mobs of sheep, warily watching the man sitting astride the big horse and his canine heart had been filled with hatred. It had been the rough treatment he had received at this man's hands which had made him fly at him, the dirty hair bristling at the neck, his eyes flashing defiance and with his teeth bared. The man had sworn at him and flung him with brutal force into the side of the road, and the dog had crawled painfully into the shelter of the ramp where he had lain for the past two days. This was the first time in his life that anyone had touched him so gently, the first time he had heard a voice speak to him with kindness, and he responded to it swiftly, licking Jean's hand and wagging his long tail, even allowing her to lift his emaciated body in her arms.

Jean carried him to the front of the car where she could see him in the headlights and stood there defiantly, looking at the man beside her.

"Is there a vet in the district?" she asked quietly.

"No."

"Is there anyone who could attend to it for me?"

He looked at her in return, that level glance she was becoming to know so well, taking in the quivering of her lips, and glancing at the torn and dusty dress which had been so pretty, and he shrugged his shoulders.

"You don't intend to keep it, do you? It looks half dead to me."

"I'm not asking what it looks like. Is there anyone who can do something for it? That's what I want to know." There was a note in her voice which made him stare, and Marie frowned. When Jean spoke like that she was really annoyed and definitely on the warpath; nothing and nobody would distract her from her purpose. She hesitated, wanting to say that this was neither the time nor the place to start arguing about dogs and that she would like to continue their journey and go home to bed. It was a decrepit-looking thing to start with, thin and starved, and pity stirred in her heart as Marie moved nearer to her daughter.

"Yes, surely there's someone around here who could do

77

something," she agreed decisively for once. "It can't be left in this state."

"It would be far better dead," argued Rob.

Jean set her lips. "I asked you –" she began again, and he turned towards the car.

"Oh, if you insist!" he answered angrily. "There's a chap who attends to animals, he lives about six miles away –"

"Take me to him, please. I can't do anything myself and the sooner the poor thing has attention the better."

"At this time of night?" he asked incredulously.

"Does it matter what time it is? If you had a broken leg you'd expect attention no matter what the hour."

"And who are you to give me orders?" he wanted to know. Jean refused to answer that, her eyes continued to hold his and Rob was the first to turn his head. "And if Mike can fix it what do you intend to do with it?" he waved towards the dog, obviously feeling that he was getting the worst of this, and Jean, sensing that the sudden movement frightened the little beast, held him tighter in her arms.

"Keep it, of course. What else?"

Mike proved to be a half-caste, a man in his early fifties, and neither his dark expressive face nor his demeanour showed any signs of annoyance about being disturbed at such an hour of the night by a request to attend to an injured dog. In the light of a hurricane lamp they all gathered round a small table which was in the centre of the hut. It was a bare room and had no comforts of any description, but Mike would have been the first to say he had no need of them; he was out from dawn to dusk and he slept for the rest of the time. He glanced from Rob's face to that of the girl and his deep brown eyes twinkled a little as he took the dog with steady gentle hands.

After a quick yet thorough examination, during which time the animal lay still, his nose resting on the palm of

Jean's hand, the half-caste gave his verdict in a low confident voice.

"No break, merely a very bad sprain. He's hungry, too. You can attend to him yourself, missie, if you have the time and the patience." And he touched the dog's head with earth-stained fingers.

"Thank you." Her face was lit by a delightful smile. "Of course I'll look after him."

"So we came all this way for nothing," remarked Rob.

"We did not," Jean contradicted him flatly. "We found out what was the matter –"

"You did. I'm not interested."

"Oh! Oh, let's go home." She brushed past him, pausing in the doorway, wondering how she could repay this man's kindness and if he would be offended if she offered him money. She was relieved when Rob saw her hesitation and came, rather unwillingly, to her rescue.

"I'll square everything with Mike later," he said in a low voice.

The half-caste followed them down the path with the hurricane lamp and halted beside the door of the car.

"How's the polo ponies you bought coming along, Mr. Rob?" he inquired with interest.

"Good, thanks," he said, and the noise of the engine drowned any further conversation.

Marie, who had the window down, shouted, "Good night and thank you," and as the lamp light died away there was a strained silence in the car.

"Polo ponies," murmured Jean wonderingly. "I haven't seen any about. Or don't I know the difference between those and an ordinary horse?"

"Probably not."

"I know many things are different up here, including the way some people treat dogs –" her voice was scornful and angry. "But I'm not so stupid as to believe you would play polo on a farm horse!"

The car stopped with a violent jerk and Jean interlocked her fingers and with her heart beating rapidly sank back in her seat, despite her anger. What had got into her tonight? She made pointed remarks to Valerie and seemed to be doing her best to make Rob lose his temper altogether.

"Who said I did? Who said I played polo at all?"

"Why have ponies if you don't?" asked Jean reasonably. "Why are you, an employee at Peppertree Lane privileged to such an extent that you can afford to buy polo ponies when poor Uncle has to scrimp and save to buy machinery for the property?"

"Why?" In the darkness Jean could not see the expression on his face because there was no dashboard light. In any case she was too busy soothing the dog who had started to tremble at the sound of the angry voices. "Because my father when he died left me a little money," he explained carefully. "And as I haven't spent all of what I've earned while working at Peppertree Lane I bought two polo ponies, because I like riding and also like playing polo. Does that explain everything to your satisfaction?"

"I beg your pardon," said Jean stiffly, wondering why she had got herself into this. If he'd been more understanding about the dog, she thought, I shouldn't feel so exasperated with him.

"Pop kindly lets me graze them on the place without charge," he added, and she clenched a small fist.

As Rob started the car again she relaxed and for the rest of the long journey home there was silence. A light, shaded by the vines, welcomed them as they neared the house. Pop was still waiting for them, perhaps wondering if the old bomb had given up the ghost at last.

He was sitting in his usual chair, in his pyjamas and slippers, and his eyes looked tired. Jean felt it was her fault that they had kept him up when he should have been in bed and as she went on to the veranda she smiled apologetically.

She would tell him what happened before Rob had a chance to speak. "I'm sorry we're so late, Uncle, it's entirely my fault. I found this on my way home and as I thought it had a broken leg I insisted that Rob should take me to have it attended to." Pop was looking at her with respect. Not many people insisted with Rob. "We had to turn back and visit a man called Mike –"

"I know him. Good chap with animals." He looked keenly at the scrap of fur cringing in her arms. "Good cattledog, that." Her face cleared at the kindliness in his voice. "Tell me about it."

He told her he was interested in what had happened, for he had waited to hear her account of the visit to the Millers and as time had passed he had started to worry and had reached the point of setting out to see if they were walking home. So while her mother sat down wearily in her chair, thinking that in less than six hours she would have to be up and about again, busy in the kitchen, Jean moved across the veranda and knelt beside the old man's chair, her fingers still moving caressingly over the dirty head of the dog she had rescued.

"If I can get him better, wash him and make him look respectable, can I – can I keep him?" she pleaded. This was the first definite request she had made of him.

"See no reason why not," said Pop. "Put it in the kitchen with the lamb."

"*Lamb?*" cried three voices in unison.

"Nigel's. Found it this evening. Motherless. He's going to feed it with a bottle." Marie's face was a picture and Jean lowered her eyes quickly before she could see the laughter in them. A lamb in her kitchen, in the room she had slaved over to make it clean and decent!

"You'd better give it more warm milk before you go to bed, Marie," he said, heaving himself up out of the chair, "while Jean attends to the dog."

"But – Gerald!" Marie started to protest that this was

81

too much, she had no idea how to feed lambs, and in any case she was rather frightened of sheep and cows. Then the habit of years made her add, "Yes, of course. If you say so, Gerald."

As the light was switched on the lamb, who had been placed in a large wooden box near the warmth of the stove and covered with a blanket by Nigel's loving hands, raised its head hopefully and indicated in no uncertain voice that it was quite ready to be fed. Jean glanced at her mother's face.

"It looks so helpless, doesn't it?" she asked gently, and Marie nodded. It did look small and helpless, as did the dog, who was being put to bed on the other side of the fire-place.

"We shall have a zoo here before long," she answered with a catch in her voice, and from the doorway, where he had been watching these proceedings, Rob nodded.

"Too true. Pop has just announced that he's promised Nigel a horse, and there's also a jar of tadpoles on the veranda."

He doesn't sound too annoyed about it either, thought Jean wonderingly as she held out a bowl of milk towards the dog. Nigel misses all the retorts and remarks which are directed against Mother and myself. Why? Is it because we're women, because we've been making, or trying to make, some alterations and improvements here and Nigel isn't interested?

Rob was almost smiling as he watched Marie gingerly hold out a bottle towards the lamb who took the rubber teat in its mouth and sucked it convincingly.

When the mail man drove out these days the bag was not allowed to be flung on one side and forgotten. Both Marie and her daughter received letters by each post and as it was not delivered every day they naturally expected to have them immediately, consequently Pop always unlocked the bag with them standing eagerly nearby, and sorted out the contents. On the Thursday afternoon after the man had left in the usual swirl of dust he obligingly upended it on the veranda table and left Jean to sort out all it contained. Later he opened his own correspondence and Rob, glancing over the top of the previous day's local paper, noticed that he was frowning.

"Anything wrong, Pop?" he inquired at once, putting down the paper and leaning forward for his packet of cigarettes and matches.

"Dunno. Maybe." Pop scratched his white hair thoughtfully, then ran his finger down his nose. He looked furtively round to make sure he and his foster-son were alone and could not be overheard. "Those investments. Remember I gave Rory Houton a cheque last time he was here? It was all in order, but now something has gone wrong."

"With the cheque or with Rory?"

"Neither. The investments," explained Pop patiently. He tapped the letter with a thick forefinger. "They want me to visit 'em. Say it will be best if I do, matter's too long to explain by mail. I'll say! I want to know what they're going to do with my money!" He stuck out his chin and glared at Rob from beneath his thick eyebrows.

"Well, what's to stop you going?" asked the other, blowing smoke rings and idly watching them drift across the veranda. "It's a long time since you went away."

"I know. Don't want to go either, for there's Marie and the children. Don't like leaving them. It's a bit lonely out here, you know."

Rob laughed. "Come off it, Pop. That's a poor excuse, they're on their own all day, you only come in for meals so they won't miss you so much. Anyway, I'm here, what more could they want?"

Pop snorted impolitely. "A lot of notice you take of 'em, son! You make your dislike of them being here very apparent at times."

The paper was flung impatiently on to the floor and Rob sat up straighter in his chair.

"I don't see that that has anything to do with you going away if you want to. I admit that I've never liked the idea and I do resent them being here, making everything different and spoiling all our bachelor ways, but it has nothing to do with this." He waved his hand towards the letter which had brought the furrows to the old chap's face. He did not like to see him worried and it was not usual for such a thing to upset him, it must be serious. "How much money is involved?"

"Ten thousand," said Pop despondently. "I was saving it for my old age."

Rob gave a shout of laughter and Jean, in her room, frowned at the sound of it. Never, in the weeks she had been here, had she seen him smile at her – at Nigel, yes, but it always faded when he looked in her direction. He had a pleasant laugh too; a great pity they did not hear more of it. Laughter and cheerfulness were so necessary to make life worth while; if it wasn't for her young brother there would not be very much to laugh at and no one to laugh with out here.

"Chickenfeed," went on Rob, still laughing.

"That's what you think," retorted the other. "But ten thousand pounds is ten thousand pounds and I'm *not* going to be diddled out of either it or the interest it would earn. I suppose because it's such a large sum they want to see me personally about it. Should have thought of that and not given the cheque to Rory with verbal instructions. Very remiss of me." He was silent for a few minutes and Rob knew better than to interrupt, then he made up his mind. "Hang it, I *will* go to Sydney and square it up right. You're quite capable of carrying on here for a few days." He stood up and stretched his big arms above his head. "Ring up and see if you can reserve a seat for me on tomorrow morning's plane. If you can't I'll have to go by train. *Marie!*"

There was a sudden scuffle from the kitchen and as he gathered up his letters his sister-in-law came running obediently, still with the lamb's milk bottle in her hand.

"Yes, Gerald?"

"I have to go away in the morning." He waved the letters towards her. "Urgent. Shan't be back until the middle of next week. Have I plenty of clean clothes?"

"Why, yes, Gerald. We washed only yesterday, we had to, Nigel gets so very dirty and as the copper was on – it's such a huge thing and it does seem a shame to waste all that hot water – I did everything else as well. Jean ironed them this afternoon. It's nothing serious, I hope?" She looked at him anxiously.

"Could be," he replied. "Pack me a case, please, I'll have to leave very early in the morning. You should know what I'll need."

"Yes, Gerald."

She hurried away and he scowled at her retreating back. "Yes, Gerald," he mimicked. "Wouldn't it have been a change if she'd turned round and said, 'Pack the damn thing yourself'?"

Marie was up earlier than usual the following morning to prepare a good breakfast before their drive to Dubbo. There had been no vacancies left on the plane and Pop had resigned himself to the thought of an all-day train journey. He busied himself throughout the meal with instructions and suggestions. Rob listened with only half his attention; he could run the whole place on his own and Pop knew it.

"Gerald." His sister-in-law came hesitatingly towards him just before he was ready to leave. "Do you think you would have time to buy one or two things while you're in the city?"

"Such as which?" Pop had visions of being asked to

85

match silks or hanks of wool, or to choose materials, and he could not imagine walking through any of the large stores with patterns of this or that in his hands. Marie held out two pieces of paper and a few dollar notes.

"We need some mixing bowls and some smaller saucepans. These –" she pointed to a cutting from a newspaper, "are what I would like if you could get them. The saucepans we have here are too big and there's only one mixing bowl that's of any use. They could be sent on by train, you would only have to order and pay for them. The money," she looked at him timidly, "I've saved that from the housekeeping allowance you've given me. The things are for the house, so it's all right, isn't it?"

"I'll get them for you," he said a trifle gruffly, and pocketed the money.

Jean watched them go from the veranda. She was still in her nightdress and would not venture further, and as the old bomb vanished from sight she gave a little hop, skip and a jump. With Uncle in Sydney and Rob, as he had told her away, for the weekend in Murra Creek, what couldn't she do with her time? Later she discovered that Jack had gone also, plus the old bomb. Sam volunteered the information that the mechanic had been given instructions to take the car through to Dubbo as well and wait until certain repairs had been effected, and she wondered shrewdly if Rob had done that on purpose.

Sam followed her into the machinery shed. "Were you wanting something, Miss Jean?" he asked helpfully, and she darted a mischievous glance in his direction.

"Only some paint," she murmured, her glance wandering over the shelves. "Mr. Rob is coming back later, isn't he?"

"So he said. We've got to finish ploughing number seven paddock today – he says it's going to rain shortly, and after that we should be able to go ahead with the planting of the wheat."

"So he's a weather prophet too? All right, I'll come back – when he's gone too," she added under her breath.

Rob left early on the Saturday morning. Jean was still washing up when she heard the purr of an expensive car and guessed that Valerie had arrived, and she went out with the tea towel still in her hand. Valerie looked at her. The curls were in great disarray and her face was without make-up, yet there was something about her small figure which matched the clearness and the joy of the morning.

"My dear, you look like somebody's slave," Valerie drawled, smiling at the same time.

"Rob's," said Jean, waving the tea towel. "His breakfast things."

"Oh!" Valerie's eyes narrowed a little and she changed the subject, apparently not at all liking the idea of Jean being Rob's slave. When Rob proposes to Valerie, Jean thought with satisfaction, she'll have the pleasure of washing that man's breakfast dishes. "I hear Pop has gone away too," Valerie went on.

Jean nodded demurely. "We're going to have a nice quiet weekend and we're rather looking forward to it. I have many letters to write and Nigel has made me promise to take him down to the river, we're going fishing. For tadpoles," she added, and the other girl shuddered daintily, smiling suddenly as Rob came down the path and flung his weekend case on the back seat. She moved over and he slid in behind the wheel.

"You'll be all right," he stated to Jean in rather a superior tone of voice.

"Quite all right. Please don't let the thought of us being alone spoil your weekend."

He compressed his lips. "I shan't! But if anything does go wrong you can leave a message with Mrs. Miller."

"Thank you."

He looked at her suspiciously as she stood by the gate with the sunlight glinting on her hair and with the tea towel wafting about in her hand. Jean smiled at him again and suddenly he felt he should not be going away; he was convinced she was up to something. Glancing round, he wondered what she could do, then Valerie gently touched his knee and he put out his hand towards the self-starter.

"Enjoy yourselves," called Jean as they moved away, "and don't forget you promised me some tennis next week, Valerie."

The other girl nodded, waved and with scarcely a sound the car moved down through the lane of peppertrees and Jean waited until the swirl of dust had settled in the distance and gave a deep contented sigh.

"Nigel!" Running round the side of the house she found him as she had expected to with the lamb, who now wore a thin piece of leather like a collar round his thin neck, and the dog, who had been nicknamed Scruffy because that was what he looked like. The dog leapt towards her and she fondled his head; he was still weak, but after many good meals, a few baths and some energetic brushing on her part, he was beginning to show signs of developing into a grand dog and it was obvious he thought the world of her with Nigel coming a close second. "Nigel! Would you like to earn a dollar?"

Her brother looked at her suspiciously. "Work, you mean?"

"In a way. How would you like to rub down the front gate and then paint it over with white undercoat?"

"Oh, I'd like that," his eyes brightened. "Can I start now?"

"You can," promised his sister. "The sandpaper is rolled up in brown paper on the kitchen table and when you've rubbed the gate smooth and got off all those flakes of old paint, then I'll give you the undercoat. And don't let the lamb or the dog put hairs on it either!"

CHAPTER SEVEN

STANDING with his hands on his hips, his hat on the back of his head which was inclined one way as he thoughtfully surveyed the fence, Sam gave his verdict. "You know, Miss Jean, if those lantana bushes there were cut back they would make the place look a whole lot tidier." He turned to survey the overhanging peppers. "And if they were hacked back a bit it would make another difference."

"I quite agree." Jean was standing by his side watching as Nigel, who was in his element, carefully daubed the gate with the white undercoat. Sam had wandered up from the men's quarters during course of the morning to inquire if there was anything the ladies were needing or if there was anything he could possibly do for them as the present moment was his own. Two of the other men had gone into town with Jack and were staying the weekend. He remarked that Mr. Rob had been exceedingly generous and had even encouraged them to go, consequently there was not much to do. He had halted in surprise at the sight of the small boy energetically rubbing down the last of the woodwork with sandpaper and had stayed to watch, at Nigel's request, the first application of paint. "And not before time," he had muttered.

"I'll cut them down if you like, Miss Jean," he offered, waving his hands towards the bushes and the trees. "I'm sure the others will help too, if you want."

"That's very good of you, Sam," she said with a grateful sigh. "I would like to surprise Uncle when he returns home." And Rob, she added to herself. He would see what a girl and a paintbrush and a bit of energy could do to make the outside of Peppertree Lane look presentable!

Within ten minutes three obliging men were busy trimming the lantana bushes and Marie, after fluttering round and asking many times if Jean was sure it would be all right, and if Uncle Gerald would have consented to this mutilation of his property, had finally offered to make morning tea and so save them the bother of trailing back to their own quarters and lighting the fire again. They all nodded and accepted her offer and then returned to their self-imposed jobs with increased vigour. Jean felt a pang as she watched the growing pile of green leaves, flowers and twigs on the ground. It was so long since the bushes had been trimmed that to get them into shape meant exposing the bare branches underneath and they did not look very pretty.

By lunchtime they had finished, and Nigel, very generously bespattered with white spots, was putting the finishing touches to the gate. Already it looked very different, and when he had put down his paintbrush he withdrew with his mother and sister to a distance to survey the change from a better angle.

"Decidedly neater," murmured his mother with her head on one side. "Gerald is sure to like it. I sincerely hope so, anyway!"

"It looks cleaner and tidier altogether," agreed Jean, looking round critically.

"My paint on the gate looks good, don't you think so?" asked Nigel proudly, and because he had made a good job of it Jean promised he could do some more another time.

"Let me do the green paint," he pleaded, and she shook her head.

"No. That's my job, I thought of it and I'm going to do it." And then when the bubbles burst she would be the one to take the blame. She was not going to say, "Oh, Nigel did it, not me!" She would confess cheerfully and defy both her uncle and Rob to find fault. Uncle Gerald would not mind, she was certain of that, for hadn't he given her permission in an offhand way, as though he had not anticipated her ever doing it, and what concern was it of Rob's? He worked for the old man, as did Sam and Jack and Ben. They were all employees while she – she raised her head a little – she was Mr. Delaney's niece.

A picnic lunch sufficed them. Nigel then vanished to take the lamb and the dog for a walk towards the men's quarters, where he was a noisy and frequent visitor, and Marie decided she would lie down for half an hour. On her way to her bedroom she peeped into the room which held the large full-sized billiard table and clicked her tongue as she noticed the ashtrays which she had emptied only yesterday; they were full again and also some magazines had been carelessly thrown on to a chair where some had slipped off on to the floor.

"Rob again!" she cried. "He must have been in here last night."

"I thought I heard the balls being knocked about." Jean stopped in the doorway and remembered, as Marie emptied the ashtrays and moved the books, the red-tipped cigarette butts she had seen in here on the day of her arrival. "Do girls play billiards?"

"Not often, I should think. Perhaps they do out here, something to occupy their time in the evenings perhaps, or maybe to give their menfolk a game. Why?"

"I just wondered."

Marie picked up a cue. "I used to play in my younger days," she announced surprisingly. "Many years ago. Your father had a craze and he used to make me play with him for practice."

"Were you good at it?" Jean looked interested and her mother gave her a smiling rueful glance.

"My dear, the craze died a sudden and violent death when I beat him each time!"

"Oh! Do you think you could remember how to play?"

"I think so." Leaning over the table, Marie held the cue

91

in a professional manner and shot one ball off another into a pocket. "Yes, it would come back with practice, I'm quite sure."

"Do you think you could teach me?" asked her daughter innocently, and five minutes later there was only the sound of Marie's quiet voice giving instructions and hints and the lazy pong of the balls hitting each other to disturb the peace of the warm afternoon.

Later Jean nodded her satisfaction when she inspected the gate and found the undercoat was dry. She would get up at her usual time in the morning and paint it that nice bright cheerful green, then, while it was drying, and she hoped there would be no strong winds to blow dust all over it, she would swear Nigel to silence and take the utility to the nearest paddock free from obstructions and see what she could do. The men would be away, they were leaving early, as soon as they had milked the cows and fed the numerous fowls and other animals, and her mother was planning to try and make some curtains from a pile of damask table-cloths she had found in an old case. Marie had washed and ironed them and moaned over them at the same time; they were beautiful and it seemed such a waste to leave them on one side. Two of the largest would hang in the dining-room; if they were dyed a delicate colour Marie was quite certain they would make a vast difference to the look of the dark room. Among her many bits and pieces she had also discovered a length of red and white check gingham which Jean had intended for a dress; this she was planning to use in the kitchen. Jean knew she would be perfectly happy measuring and cutting up and would not bother about her children, especially if she saw Nigel was with his sister.

Neither felt lonely during the long evening; there were many little jobs to do that they could do better with the men out of the way. Jean washed her hair and manicured her nails, then wandered out on to the veranda and looked across the garden. Now the hedge had been trimmed and the peppers cut back it was possible to see down the track towards the river, and she wondered idly what Rob and Valerie would be doing. As far as she knew they were attending a party – Rob had not been very communicable – and tomorrow, when she was battling with the utility, if she ever got it started, they would be playing tennis.

She thought of Rob's lean brown face and wondered again why he never smiled at her, why he treated her as a necessary evil, and she frowned. He had never called her by her name, either Jean or Miss Delaney, and then the frown was replaced by a smile as she recollected the morning when he had wanted her for something and had shouted "Hi, you!" With her head in the air she had continued on her way and he had had to run after her, muttering something under his breath about the cussedness of women. Jean had stopped when he reached her, giving him a glance as leved as his own and had waited.

"Didn't you hear me call you?" he had asked.

"No." She had shaken her head definitely and made to go on her way. "I did hear you shout Hi, you, but naturally didn't think you were talking to me!"

She chuckled a little in the darkness, then her mother called that she was going to bed and she went inside, switching off all the lights one by one.

Leaving Marie contentedly measuring damask and linen, Jean led her brother from the house the following morning. Everything was quiet and Jean wondered what her mother would say and do if she heard the engine of the utility roar into life. Nigel thought it a great joke; he was naturally an observant child and was very mechanically minded. He had assured his sister in a very low whisper that he could drive the thing himself, for hadn't Bruce let him hold the wheel the other morning? There was nothing to it, he said airily, and with a pointed stick he drew a diagram of the gear changes in the dust. Jean nodded.

"I understand," she said gravely. "But is the utility the

same as the old bomb? I mean, are the gears alike on both of them?"

Nigel thought for a moment. He was not too sure on that point. "But if they're not we shall soon find out, shan't we?" he inquired brightly.

Seated behind the wheel Jean felt a tremor at her boldness. If she smashed this thing up what would Uncle have to say? For a moment her fingers played a tune on the wheel and she remembered Valerie's confident way of getting into a car and driving away, she thought of Mrs. Kennedy and decided that if she couldn't make it go she would ring Gum Valley and ask what to do. It might be wiser to do that in the first place. Then she shook herself.

"Ah, well, here goes," she sighed, and pressed the self-starter. Nothing happend.

"You haven't switched the engine on," remarked Nigel.

Jean bit her lip. Thank goodness he was the only one with her! Rob would have made some scathing remark and stared through the windscreen and she would have the feeling of being about the size of a sixpence. The key was there, she had not given it a thought, and at the next attempt the engine purred and she listened. This was in better condition than the other car which Pop used and which was the only one they had been driven in so far. Her hand rested on the gear lever. Nigel watched each move and nodded with approval as her foot pressed down on the clutch. Slowly the utility began to move and then stopped, its engine cutting out immediately. Three times more she tried and her face was white, then they did move forward a few yards and she had to change gear again, at the same time watch where she was going. Her mother did not appear on the veranda with anxious inquiries as to what they were doing or what was wrong, and it was with a sigh of relief that Jean turned a corner, so cutting the house from view, and was confronted by a closed gate.

"The footbrake – quick! The middle one," cried Nigel.

As they stopped with the bonnet only a bare inch or so from the large iron gate he turned to look at her anxiously. "Do you think you can manage it?"

"Of course I can! Once I get used to it. Get down and open it, there's a dear, and we'll try again."

Half an hour later the colour had returned to her face and Nigel was sitting in a more relaxed position. They had stopped and started many times, for practice, as Jean calmly informed her critical tutor, and the boy was being helpful though not always polite. Between them they had managed to discover what everything was for, the engine was still running and her nervousness was gradually leaving her.

"You haven't gone backwards yet," said her brother after they had been round the same paddock for the third time.

"All in good time, sonny boy. We're getting on fine, aren't we?"

"Not bad. But you never look in the driving mirror."

"I can't look everywhere at once!"

"You're supposed to," he said awkwardly. "Rob does."

He opened and closed many gates, swinging on some of them, and Jean became more confident; she was overcoming the noise she made when changing gear and she could start without too many jerks. In time this would come as easily and as naturally as walking and she would be able to drive into town, take her mother shopping instead of having to use the telephone, and she must call at Gum Valley, when she discovered where it was, and thank Mrs. Kennedy for putting the idea into her head.

Marie's astonishment, when she saw them drive to the gate, was ludicrous. Her mouth opened and closed as she fumbled for words and her children sat there laughing helplessly at her changing expressions.

"Jean!" her daughter realised that she did not know whether to be angry or not, for in a flash she had realised the possibilities of having her own transport into town. So her anger faded and she felt a glow of pride for this independent daughter of hers. "My dear, what have you been doing? Did Uncle give you permission?"

"No. But I'm sure he would have done if he'd been here," said Jean, stepping down stiffly from the driving seat. It was set too far back for her, she would feel much more comfortable if her feet were not stretched out so much. "Don't be cross with me, dear, but it was too good an opportunity to miss. Rob was out of the way and so were the men. Nigel has been a little angel, too – did you know he could almost drive it himself?"

"Sure I can, any time." Nigel grinned. This morning he had learnt a great deal by trial and error along with his sister.

"But you mustn't try!" cried his mother in alarm, and added anxiously, "You haven't hit anything, have you?"

"Only two sheep, one horse and a gate," answered her son, and gave a whoop of delight as her expression changed again.

Rather excitedly they went in to lunch, which had been prepared and which they ate on the veranda in the shade of the vines. Jean was flushed by her success and was perhaps overconfident; she planned another drive during the afternoon before Rob returned home and Nigel said he had no wish to accompany her again; he had taught her all he knew and could do no more, so his mother offered to take him down to the river with the lamb and fish for tadpoles as his sister was too busy. There was little more for her to do inside, the curtains were all cut out ready for sewing and until some dye had been purchased nothing else could be done with them.

The river looked cool and placid in the shadows of the afternoon and sitting on the bank, watching as Nigel wandered up and down with a bottle in one hand and a net made from a piece of mosquito netting in the other hand,

and with the lamb tethered nearby, Marie felt at peace. It was very quiet and if only she knew more people how pleasant life would be. More neighbours and more gadgets in the house, at the moment that was all she asked from life.

Jean was trying the utility again. She would have found it impossible to describe her feelings at the moment, as she stepped in and sat down in the driving seat and the engine purred into life with the movement of her finger on the self-starter. She was laughing as she careered along the two narrow tracks which led to the far side of this large paddock.

An hour later she realised she was lost. Each paddock looked more or less the same until you realised that the gum trees in one were in an opposite direction in another. There were no sheep in this one, it was merely rough grass with tufts of a coarser herbage and few thistles. The one she had driven through previously had seemed the same; now she was not sure and she stopped, frowning, as she tried to make out from which direction she had come. The utility was behaving as it should and she had overcome her first mistrust of it, but she must be miles away from the homestead – and supposing the petrol ran out? Anxiously she glanced at her wrist watch. The afternoon was still young and if she continued to drive around she would surely see something familiar and be able to find her way back.

Twice she had to stop because logs stuck out on to the track and caught at the back wheels; she had to strain and heave to lift them out of the way and returned to the driving seat conscious that she was trembling all over. The tracks appeared to double back on themselves and would disappear into the distance. Finally she came to a clump of pines and she knew she had not been this way before. The trees were straight, gave a welcome patch of shade. They looked like a myriad Christmas trees and as she stared at them she tried hard to stem back her tears. It was not a pleasant feeling being stranded in the centre of these paddocks, for she was sure in her own mind that Rob had not brought them here when he took them on that tour of inspection the day after they arrived. She might be on someone else's property, for they were all joined by wire netting fences, and she scanned the horizon, hoping to see the sun glinting on an iron roof somewhere, but there was nothing but the gum trees which looked in the distance to melt into the sky.

Going forward again because as yet she had not dared go in reverse, she went another few yards and the back wheels again hit a half-hidden log, the utility stopped of its own accord.

"May I inquire what you're playing at?" asked an icy voice at her elbow, and she spun round on her seat to see Rob, sitting astride a large white horse, his face and demeanour more angry than she had ever seen it. Relief flooded over her, she was found and no longer lost.

"I shall be playing the harp if someone doesn't remove all the obstacles from my path and take me home!" she cried, and burst into tears.

CHAPTER EIGHT

FOR a long time there were only the cries of the crows as they wheeled about overhead and the rather pathetic sound of Jean's sobbing to break that awful quiet. She had her arms bent over the steering wheel and her head rested upon them; beyond the lazy twitching of its tail the white horse stood almost motionless and its rider did not move either; the reins were held lightly in one strong hand and the other was clenched against his thigh. Rob continued to stare angrily at her, apparently quite unmoved, and as he waited for the tears to dry up the fury within him mounted steadily.

Jean was furious with herself for crying like this, but she could not stop. The tears were chiefly of relief and rage. It had been a bigger strain than she had thought possible, driving the utility without permission with only Nigel to help, then the shock of realising she was lost within these great bare paddocks, followed by Rob's totally unexpected and sudden arrival, all those things had helped to make her do something she normally scorned. Tears, she would say with vigour, were for the weak and the helpless, and she was neither.

At length the sobbing ceased and she fumbled in a pocket for a handkerchief. Not finding one, she furtively wiped her eyes on the hem of her dress and then pulled it down again over her knees. Still sniffing slightly, she turned her head slightly to see Rob still sitting in the same position and the horse appeared to be watching her with sympathy. And I shall need it, she thought grimly.

"You were supposed to be playing tennis," she remarked tremulously and rather accusingly.

"And because you presumed I should be there all day I

suppose this is the result?" he asked between his teeth.

Jean nodded, feeling better each minute. The tears had been a relief after all.

"How dare you bring the utility out here when you can't drive –"

"Oh, but I can drive. Now." She added the last word after a moment's thought.

"Who taught you? Who dared to bring you out into the paddocks without my permission?"

"I came alone." Jean was very thankful that she had not asked Sam or any of the others if they would teach her, for part of this fury would have been directed against them.

Rob looked horrified and very disbelieving. Yet she was very definitely alone. "You actually had the nerve to drive the car out here without anyone with you or without any tuition? Were you mad to try such a thing? I thought if I sent Jack away all the vehicles would be safe and you too, yet here you are on next door's property. Heaven alone knows what the engine's like by now!"

He paused for breath and Jean could see that he was trying to think of words that would bring home to her the enormity of her crime, but they would not come. Indignation, disapproval and anxiety were all bubbling up within him and the words seemed to stick in his throat.

"Why did you come home early?" she inquired with interest.

"Because I knew something would happen in my absence! I had a feeling that all was not as it should be and that it was imperative that I return –"

"What a pity you spoilt your day for nothing!"

She saw Rob hit his clenched hand against his leg, sitting more upright in the saddle, and the horse sidestepped a little restlessly.

"*Nothing!* You call it nothing? Yet the first thing that met my eyes was the green gate. That's your doing, I know it. You've been in the shed and taken the paint I had for the machinery – the bushes and trees, they've been cut back and spoiled. Then I found your mother and brother wandering back along the track from the river and you not with them. The ute is missing and Nigel announces that you've gone for a drive –"

"You're being very high-handed about all this," retorted Jean, also sitting upright in her seat and wishing she had more height to give her more dignity. "After all, as I've remarked before, it's no concern of yours. Sam doesn't query what I do, neither does Jack, nor Bruce, or Ben – you're only a paid hand here, too. Uncle gave me permission to paint the gate – you heard him, for you were there at the time. If he'd been here he would have agreed, I'm quite sure about it, to the cutting of the bushes. You must admit it makes the whole place look different altogether." She smiled at him, determined to keep her good humour. "We've been so busy this weekend."

"That's perfectly obvious! But this –!" He waved his hand violently towards the utility and the horse pranced a little. "You had no right to bring this out here. Pop didn't give his permission for you to do that, or to learn to drive."

"I meant to ask him, but he left in rather a hurry. I did ask you and you refused. Jack had been sent to Dubbo, and I guessed why." She was beginning to feel angry herself at the injustice of it all. If Uncle Gerald had been with him, then she could have expected fireworks and would have apologised, sincerely and contritely, but she was not going to let the jackaroo tell her what or what not to do. "That was your doing too. And as I now live here I see no reason at all why I should always have to ask you or have you ordered by my uncle to drive me into town." Rob flushed. "And now I think we'll return home."

Her hand moved towards the self-starter and Rob looked at her.

101

"Didn't you know you had a flat tyre?"

Her face paled a little and she wondered wildly for a moment if there was anything else that had gone wrong.

"What are you going to do about it?" he asked rather mockingly, and she swallowed hard.

"You'll – you'll have to show me what to do," she said, and it hurt her pride.

Slowly he dismounted and tied the reins to the front bumper bar. The horse snorted a little and Jean looked at it; it was a very beautiful animal and she remembered seeing it in one of the paddocks with some others and had admired it, for it was pure white and had not another mark upon it. Was it one of the polo ponies? she wondered as she stepped down.

"You know, Rob, it would have saved a great deal of trouble and a lot of unpleasantness if you hadn't been so rude and snapped my head off when I asked you, in a very polite manner, if I could learn to drive. Then this wouldn't have happened and your weekend wouldn't have been spoilt."

"The spare is in the back," was the only reply she received, and as she clambered in and put her hands on the heavy tyre she knew that he was going to make her change it herself. Part of her punishment, she thought wonderingly. What a man! "The spanners and the jack are there too."

Rob leaned against the side of the utility and calmly lit a cigarette as he gave instructions, Jean followed them faithfully, knowing this was a reprisal and she was unable to argue about it; unless the wheel was changed she would not get back to the homestead. And Rob in his present mood would be quite capable of leaving her to find her own road home. Anyway, she consoled herself, it was something worth knowing; there might come a time when she could be stranded upon the road from Murra Creek and as passing vehicles were not plentiful on that road, she might sit helplessly in the sun and the dust for a couple of hours before someone came along, and then it might be another woman who would, in all probability, be as helpless as she. It was hard work and the large nuts on the jacked-up wheel were tightly screwed. Perspiration glistened on her forehead and in pushing back her hair she left a long greasy streak upon her cheek. Gritting her teeth, determined not to ask for assistance, for she could be as stubborn as he, she struggled with the unwieldy spanner, and at the moment when Rob decided he had better give in and go to her assistance, she loosened the first nut. There was a knack in it, Jean discovered, and the others followed quickly, then the tyre swung free and she was able to lift it down.

In perfect silence she rolled it away and left it to fall on the grass and the other was moved nearer to the jacked-up wheel. Heaving grimly, she lifted it; it slipped and fell on her foot. She stepped back quickly, still retaining her hold upon it, then the wheel was taken from her and Rob hitched it up into position.

"Stubborn little fool, aren't you?" he muttered, reaching for the spanner. The nuts were tightened and the jack was let down, another twist to them all, then he slung the spanners, the flat tyre and the jack carelessly into the back of the utility where they would stay until Jack noticed them or he remembered to have the tyre mended.

Jean moved round to the driving seat and he spun round. "What are you going to do now?" he asked, looking at her heated stained face.

"Drive home. What else? You have your horse."

"But —" he had intended doing that himself, with the horse trotting behind, but she was seated now and he knew she would not come out unless he lifted her down.

"You'll have to show me the way, of course."

"Haven't you any idea where you are?"

"None at all, I'm afraid. These paddocks are so huge, many of them look alike. I opened and closed so many

103

gates and honestly don't know how far I am from home."

"You're in the next property, thirteen miles from Peppertree Lane," he said grimly.

She was surprised. "As far as that? However did you find me?" she asked curiously, thinking it was lucky he had. If she had gone on driving away from the river as she had been doing she might have missed Murra Creek altogether and finished up, when the petrol finally did run out, across at Peak Hill or somewhere like that. For the first time she realised what a huge area the Western Districts covered.

"Nigel pointed vaguely in this direction. Then I saw the dust. It's such a still afternoon it lingers in the air." He had seen it in the distance and made his way rapidly across the paddocks in that direction, taking short cuts of his own and jumping fences, then he had heard, in the stillness of the warm afternoon, the revving of the engine and had finally seen the utility as it crawled out of the pine trees.

"I suppose that in time I shall come to know every inch of these paddocks," she remarked as he walked round to untie the reins and the horse pranced back. Jean looked him straight in the face.

"I shall naturally tell Uncle all about it," she announced quietly, and he shrugged his shoulders.

"Which way do we go?" Jean was smiling at him quite pleasantly, but if she had hoped he would smile back she was disappointed and slowly she pressed the self-starter. It would have been gratifying to have had a smile in reply and to feel she was forgiven her misdemeanours, for the smile so often flashed in Nigel's direction was an attractive one. She sighed gently as the engine purred and she waited.

Rob swung himself up into the saddle and moved away. The girl hesitated, hoping desperately that she would get away to a smooth start without any of the horrid jerks which had attended her starts previously. She could im-

104

agine the way he would cringe at the sound she made and tightened her lips.

"Ah, perfect take-off!" she murmured with satisfaction as she moved off after the white horse, and Rob shook his head in bewilderment. She changed gear like a professional and Rob broke into a canter, having no desire to be left to follow in the dust.

Marie and Nigel were waiting anxiously by the newly painted gate as the utility with its escort came into view and Marie sighed. Jean was still whole, and she was truly thankful about that fact as she remembered the look on Rob's face when Nigel calmly announced that his sister was driving out there somewhere and had waved towards the distant horizon. Without a word he had walked from them and when next she had seen him he was on the back of a white horse, and even in her anxiety she had stopped to admire the perfect picture they made together.

"If only I could ride like that!" Nigel had exclaimed wistfully.

"It will come in time if you're careful," murmured his mother absently, still watching Rob. He had not bothered to stop by the gate, the reins had tightened and he bent low, the horse gathered up his feet and leapt over the closed gate with ease.

"Showing off," remarked the boy, and she had had to laugh.

As she got out of the car Jean glanced at the tight-lipped face of the man swinging himself down from the saddle and she straightened herself. What right had he to be annoyed with her for what she had done? Granted he was in charge of Peppertree Lane during the owner's absence in Sydney, but he was not in charge of the occupants of the house.

"I became lost," Jean stood before her mother, one hand reaching for Scruffy's head as he whined and whimpered with the excitement of seeing her again and announced the other of her faults immediately: "Then I had a flat tyre.

Then Rob came along and everything was all right again," finished the girl blandly.

"I'm glad of that," answered her mother. "Because when he left here he looked as though he could cheerfully murder you! I gathered that the cleaning up we did here yesterday and today were not too popular." Away from her brother-in-law Mrs. Delaney was not intimidated. The owner of this property with his huge thickset body and abrupt way of speaking rather frightened her, but not Rob. She thought, as did her daughter, that he was merely an employee and she was taking orders from no one during Gerald's absence. Advice, yes, that was an entirely different matter, and there were many things she was still very uncertain about and which she would like to know more.

Rob scowled at her. He paused by the gate and found Mrs. Delaney beside him.

"I'll explain all this to my brother-in-law when he returns home," she said quietly, and then went on to announce firmly, "I want some cream and red paint, enamel if possible, from the machinery shed – oh, we shan't use much," she added hastily as she saw the mutinous look in his eyes, and rather spoilt the effect of the stand she was making. "It's only for the cupboards in the kitchen. And I also want something from town tomorrow. Can one of the men drive in and get what I need? Jean isn't experienced enough yet– "

"I'll say she isn't! There's a great deal that girl will have to learn before she can go into Murra Creek alone. Why have you to start painting in the kitchen, may I ask? It always looked all right to me!"

"It hasn't been done for goodness knows how many years!" cried Marie with exasperation. "It's dingy and I don't like it. If I have to spend hours in there cooking your meals I want the place to look bright and attractive. Let me have it as soon as you can, please." And she swept up the path, shepherding Nigel before her leaving Rob staring at her straight back. So Marie was standing on her dignity now!

Nigel was sent into the machinery shed later for the paint. Rob was there carefully scrutinising the utility and the boy smiled.

"You won't find any marks, if that's what you're looking for," he said confidently. "We didn't hit anything."

"We?" Rob straightened his back.

"Sure. I went with Jean and showed her what to do. The gears, you know. She had little idea to start with," answered Nigel proudly. "I think I'll be able to drive it myself very soon."

"You'll do no such thing! Keep away from the machinery and the tractors and everything! Do you hear? I won't have you meddling with these things, they cost too much money —"

Nigel sat down on a petrol tin and cupped his chin in his hands. "I suppose they do. That's where all Uncle's money goes, isn't it? Jean says so anyway. You know, I thought it would be much better out here than it is in some ways, because we all believed Uncle had lots and lots of money. But I like him even when he hasn't," he added very staunchly. "And I do like living here now I've got the lamb and the pony, and do you think we could get a wallaby or a baby kangaroo somewhere? Ben was telling me about a boy he knew up in the Territory, he'd even a little alligator as a pet!" Nigel's eyes grew round at the thought of it and he sighed regretfully because there were no such things to be found in the Macquarie. "Can I have that paint, please? The red and cream? Mummy is going to let me do some too after school tomorrow, I helped Jean with the gate this morning. We're painting the cupboards cream and putting the red about to brighten it up. I like red, don't you?"

"I'll be seeing red soon!" Rob muttered, going slowly towards where the paint was kept.

During the evening Valerie rang and, contrary to expectation, she did not sound annoyed at Rob's early departure from her home. She was sweet and understanding.

"Oh, I can well understand Rob's anxiety," she told Jean. "It must be a responsibility for him. Leaving you alone – you aren't used to it, dear, and must have been quite jittery –"

"No, that's not the word I should use," replied Jean thoughtfully.

"What have you been doing with yourselves? Have you managed all right?" Valerie asked curiously.

"Yes, we've kept ourselves well occupied." She had no intention of explaining all that had happened in Rob's absence.

She gave an exaggerated sigh of relief. "Oh, about the tennis. You sounded rather keen, so I've arranged a little game for you next Wednesday if that will suit you. Rob can tell you where the courts are."

Jean turned from the phone and wandered out on to the veranda. Nigel was there with a train set; numerous lines wound themselves across the clean bare boards, under chairs, and a beautiful loop encircled the sleeping cattle dog. Scruffy was an interested spectator and Jean saw that Rob had paused on his way outside to admire the little engine, to be informed that he was standing on Murra Creek station and would he please step back? He did so hastily, glancing down towards his feet. Jean smiled.

"But there's no station there!"

"It's an imaginary one. Like where Bess is lying, that's the trucking yard. I used to have some little stations," the boy stood a signal near a chair leg, "but I think Mummy must have thrown them out when we were packing up, I can't find them anywhere. Daddy bought me this set for my birthday."

Kneeling down to watch the performance, Rob became interested, for the engine and numerous coaches and trucks

108

were good ones and it was years since he had played with trains. Nigel remarked that it was rather awkward when all the stations were in his mind's eye, so he didn't always stop in quite the same place.

"I'll make you one or two," offered the man suddenly. "Let's go into the shed, I know where there are some pieces of plywood."

They left the veranda together and returned over an hour later with three wooden stations which satisfied Nigel because of their perfect symmetry. As Rob knelt again to help arrange them he stiffened suddenly. Surely someone was in the billiard room?

"Who's that?" he asked sharply, and Nigel also listened. He smiled, relaxed, and moved another station near the sleeping dog.

"Mummy and Jean. They're playing billiards."

"They're *what*?"

"Playing billiards," repeated the boy, removing the dog's paw from across the line. "They play a lot while you and Uncle are out."

"Oh, for Pete's sake, what next? The baize –" Rob hurried into the house.

The door was flung open and he stopped at the sight of Marie, who had her back towards him, hitting the ball straight off another into a pocket. Jean was at the other end of the table, chalking the end of her cue, and she smiled as she noticed him.

"Come on in, Rob," she invited. "Perhaps you would like to have a game too?"

Five minutes later, when her mother was hurrying Nigel off to bed, Jean sat down and laughed until the tears ran down her face. The piano was being thumped hard and one of Sousa's marches was being well and truly murdered.

CHAPTER NINE

THE dyeing of the curtains was a great success and Jean had cause to feel justly proud of her handiwork. She had telephoned through to the store in Murra Creek, explaining carefully and exactly what she needed, and Jack had been instructed, also by telephone by Rob, to call in at the store on his way home from Dubbo, so saving someone a journey into town from Peppertree Lane. Within a couple of hours of his return the damask was being attended to in one of the deep tubs in the laundry and soon the curtains were flapping about in the breeze on the long line and Jean was cleaning the windows and the surrounding paintwork in the dining-room ready to receive them.

"I can't believe it," whispered Marie a little while later, as she surveyed the draperies with shining eyes. "They make the room!"

Jean smiled, admitting she would not have believed curtains could make such a great difference. They hung to the floor, stiff and heavy, gleaming a little in the electric light which had been switched on, a rose shade which seemed to vary in depth and beauty because of the markings of the damask. Slowly she spun round on her high heels, critically eyeing everything. The large sheepskin rug before the fireplace had been washed and was now a snowy white; the furniture, all highly polished, reflected her swirling figure, as did the floor, and the table with its vases of roses and trailing greenery of asparagus fern and laid preparatory for dinner was an invitation in itself. Now they could invite Mrs. Miller, all the *élite* of Murra Creek, even the Governor of the Bank of England, she thought recklessly, and would have no cause to feel ashamed of anything in here. This could not be improved upon and she gave a deep sigh.

Surely Pop would be pleased; he could not possibly be anything else, for it had cost him nothing. All she had spent had been the few cents for the dye, the cost of the tins of polishing wax and the soap which had naturally come out of her housekeeping money.

With her mother's arm around her shoulders Jean walked through into the lounge and a frown gathered between her eyes.

"This is a large and stately room, but there's something missing," she said definitely. "It's so dull and uninviting and I doubt if the new curtains will improve it as much as the others have done in the dining-room." She glanced round thoughtfully; the room was tidy and clean; there were many vases of flowers in here too and the small coffee table which she had discovered in one of the other rooms, a heavy little table made of solid jarrah, had upon it a silver cigarette box and a couple of books. The piano was open and Jean wandered across to it, her fingers lightly touching the keys. As she did so she wished Rob would entertain them one evening in a proper manner instead of always demonstrating his skill with bursts of angry sounds which, though musical, were rather too loud and tiring to the nerves to listen to for any length of time.

"No," agreed her mother. "It's still lacking in something."

They both stared round the room, at the high ceilings which had been swept bare of numerous cobwebs, and the large windows, then Marie gave an exclamation.

"It's the old suite," she cried. "That's what spoils it. It wants throwing out!"

"We should have nothing to sit on if you did that," answered her daughter, sitting down in one of the chairs and stretching out her legs. "It's very comfortable, the trouble is that I feel lost in a chair of this size. Oh, I wish I was taller!"

"Why? You'd only be gawky," said her mother absently.

111

Then her face cleared and she smiled. "Loose covers! They're the only solution. Oh, Jean, do you think we could make some?"

Jean scrambled to her feet and glanced at the large chairs and even larger settee. "What an idea! Of course they're the obvious thing! You get some wonderful brain-waves at times, dear."

"Covers would hide the shabbiness," went on Marie eagerly. "If we chose something to match the curtains, per-haps a deeper shade so they wouldn't show the dirt so quickly – men just come in and sit down forgetting that a few minutes before they were sitting in a saddle or in that old bomb which I'm sure has never been properly cleaned since it was new, and that's many years ago. And Nigel – you know what he is! He needs clean pants each hour of the day when he's playing outside. Oh, do you think we could possibly do it?"

"I'm sure we could," said the girl thoughtfully, running her hands over the arms and the backs of the chairs. "No springs gone, they're solid enough. But you'd need yards and yards of material, and what should we use to buy it with?"

Marie shrugged her shoulders. "Money, my love. And I haven't any left from the housekeeping this month. I gave it all to your uncle to buy those saucepans and things we really do need. Oh, what a nuisance! We'll have to wait for ages until I've saved up enough, and now I've started doing all these things I feel just in the mood to carry on. I almost wish Gerald was staying away for weeks and then I could present him with a brand new house upon his return and show him that I'm not quite as silly as he seems to think I am! I only hope he doesn't mind what I've done to his tablecloths."

"He must have forgotten they were there – they hadn't been disturbed for years, judging by the condition they were in. How many are left? Could we do anything with

112

the ones you didn't use for curtains?"

"I doubt it," said her mother gloomily. "That's such a large settee and I don't think I would like a plain colour and we couldn't dye it in patches, that would look amateurish and odd! No, I shall just have to wait, that's all. There's Rob and Nigel – just listen to them laughing!"

Nigel gets it again, thought Jean, listening to the merriment that was coming from the direction of the veranda, and when I go in there his whole expression will change, his mouth will tighten as though it's an effort to keep back words he longs to say. He'll look over me, which isn't difficult, through me and round me. Whatever have I done to deserve being ignored like this? It's been the same ever since the first day we arrived.

"Call Nigel, dear. I want him to fetch me some lemons, he does love going into the orchard."

Rob was the first to enter the dining-room, for he was very hungry.

Halfway through the door he stopped.

"They look nice, don't you think so?" asked a quiet voice behind him.

"Um!" It was a very noncommittal answer; he was not going into raptures about new curtains with Jean. "Where did you get them?"

"Mother found some tablecloths in an old suitcase. She washed them, dyed them and behold –" she waved her hands. "Curtains!"

"Which old suitcase?" he asked suspiciously.

"One we discovered on the bottom shelf of what's now the linen cupboard," explained the girl patiently. "And judging by the numbers of cobwebs which clung between it and the wall it hadn't been touched for years."

Rob frowned. It had to be admitted that all these two women had done had certainly been an improvement. He glanced along the white cloth, looking at the silver and the flowers – there were even table napkins these days.

113

Jean knew that he approved, although grudgingly, of all the hard work that she and her mother had done.

A brief telegram arrived from Pop the following morning and even as she took the message over the telephone and laughed about its curtness, for the message contained only four words – "Not arriving Wednesday. Pop." – Jean was wondering how she would get into town to play tennis with Valerie on that afternoon. Going into her bedroom, where her white shorts and blouse were hanging, neatly pressed, and her tennis racquets had been brought out for inspection, she squirmed at the very thought of asking Rob to drive her in again. In all probability he would refuse point blank, and Uncle Gerald would not be here to order him to do it. She dare not take the utility without asking Rob's permission; in any case he would refuse, and rightly so, she admitted fairly, to use it for only the second time and drive into town, and not for one minute did she believe Jack or any of the others would be allowed to drive her. Her mother and Nigel were also going into town. Then a sudden thought crossed her mind and acting on impulse she returned to the hall and picked up the phone book.

A few minutes later she was speaking to Mrs. Kennedy at Gum Valley and surprised at herself asking if she would be driving into town on Wednesday and if so, seeing she would be passing the end of the track out from Peppertree Lane, would she mind very much if the Delaney family went with her?

"I'm playing tennis with Valerie," she ended rather breathlessly. "And Mother is taking Nigel in to have his hair cut and look round the shops –"

"As it happens I've also been invited to play with Valerie too," said the other. "And I'll call for you all with pleasure."

"That's very good of you," breathed Jean thankfully.

"How are the driving lessons proceeding? Have you managed to get out in the car at all?"

Rather ruefully the girl described her adventures in the paddocks with the utility, and as Mrs. Kennedy laughed softly Jean could almost see the amused friendliness in her eyes.

"We'll certainly have to do something about all this, Jean," she remarked. "And soon! Would you like to return, with your mother and Nigel of course, to Gum Valley for dinner on Wednesday evening? I haven't met your brother yet and I like small boys. There'll be plenty to amuse him here, we keep some toys in stock for young visitors and we've also dogs, cats and kittens –"

"Oh, no!" whispered Jean, having visions of her brother returning home with his arms full of furry bundles which he would insist had to live in the house. There were plenty of cats about here too, but they were half wild and resented the boy's efforts at friendliness with many scratches and spits in his direction, which annoyed Nigel. He wanted to add them to his growing collection of animals.

With a promise to call at Peppertree Lane about one o'clock Mrs. Kennedy rang off. Marie and Nigel were still in the schoolroom, the housework had been finished early, for they were always up and about by half past six and Jean wondered what else she could find to do to help make the old house look more presentable. She peeped into each room in turn wishing she could cover all the windows with new curtains and the floors with soft rugs, each room but Rob's, and she passed his closed door without even glancing at it. Neither her mother or herself had done anything in there. They had cleaned Pop's room and polished his furniture, rearranged his books and sorted out the many things he had flung down at one time or another in his attempts not to make the rest of the house look untidy, but by a mutual unspoken agreement they had left the jackaroo's room alone. Solely to be awkward, admitted Miss Delaney!

At lunchtime Rob came in hot and dusty, for they were

now ploughing the last of the paddocks ready for the planting of the wheat and he had been around everywhere, and without a word Jean handed him the message taken over the phone and he raised his eyebrows, wondering aloud what had made the old man decide to stay longer in Sydney. Rob explained how Pop disliked the city. There would not be a letter explaining his sudden decision. Pop would not write letters unless he was compelled to and until he returned home they would hear nothing further from him.

"And that means I can't go in to meet him," he said. "Unless he sends another wire to say which day he's arriving."

Jean waited. The arrangement, which she had taken for granted, had been that she and her mother and Nigel would go into town with Rob when he drove in to meet her uncle, and now there was not that excuse she wondered if Rob, who had personally given her the message from Valerie about playing on Wednesday afternoon, would remember and offer to take them in. She hoped he would, then she could inform him that they had made other arrangements. But he didn't; he sat down absently fingering his fork, his thoughts still out in the paddocks with the tractors and ploughs.

Nothing was said even up to Wednesday morning. Jean received the impression that Rob was ignoring the whole affair and felt furious with his casualness and indifference, forbidding Marie and Nigel to mention the subject at all. He announced at breakfast time that he would be out all day, for it was clouding over and rain was threatening. There was still much he had to do, Pop's work as well as his own. Jean compressed her lips, quite convinced he was being awkward on purpose.

She watched him stride away and turned to see her mother gazing at her.

"Why wouldn't you let me tell him we shouldn't be in

116

tonight?" Marie asked. "There won't be a meal ready for him and he'll be tired."

"Sam can cook something extra," returned her daughter shortly. "Perhaps he'll appreciate more of what we do for him if he has to return to Sam's administrations for a while."

"Yes, I see what you mean," Marie sighed. "It *would* be nice to have someone say thank you for something! All we've done here, and no one seems to appreciate it."

But when Mrs. Kennedy arrived early she had much to say about the alterations and was sincere in her praise for the way Peppertree Lane seemed to have changed for the better since she was last here.

Marie felt a surge of joy at the other woman's praise as they went into the house and she opened all the cupboards and displayed the tidy shelves with housewifely pride, thinking how pleasant it was to have someone else in the kitchen with her, someone who knew and understood the difficulties of storing sufficient food to last over a period, for she could not rush into town and buy something she had forgotten on her grocery order. Confiding that she would be more than thankful when Jean had passed her driving test and could take her shopping more often, she led the way into the dining-room and waited. Neither was she disappointed at what was said of the change in there.

"I hope Gerald likes it when he comes home. He had to go to Sydney in a hurry and we've done all this in his absence."

"He couldn't do anything else but love it," answered Mrs. Kennedy, standing back to have a good look at the curtains which had once been tablecloths. "And Rob? Does he like it too?"

"If he does he's never said so," retorted Jean, and the other darted a swift glance at the girl's face.

"But as he's only the jackaroo perhaps he feels he shouldn't pass comments," said her mother fairly, and Mrs.

Kennedy opened her mouth as if to make some comment and then closed it again quickly. Jean wondered what she had intended to say.

Nigel was first to get into the large car standing by the gate and he gave a sigh of content.

"This is the sort of car we expected Uncle to have," he remarked, surveying the dashboard with critical eyes. "But he only has the old bomb and the utility, and all those lovely tractors and things, of course. If he sold one of those he could afford to buy one of these, couldn't he?" he appealed hopefully to the world in general, and his mother made signs at him behind Mrs. Kennedy's back. It was not the thing to discuss his uncle's finances with a comparative stranger.

Mrs. Kennedy held open the door by the driving seat and looked at Jean.

"Come on," she invited. "Try this."

The girl's face paled a little. "I couldn't! Oh, I couldn't use that! I might hit something!"

"That's a risk we shall all have to take," returned the other calmly. "But you'll find it easy, more so than the one you were driving the other day, and the more practice you have the better you'll be. Get in, Jean, I'll sit beside you and tell you what to do."

Jean looked at her mother who smiled encouragingly as though to say, "You've got to learn properly some time and Mrs. Kennedy is offering you a chance you shouldn't refuse!" She looked at Nigel, who was grinning confidently. If his sister could drive the other old thing she would drive this beauty. Then she thought of Rob and slid in behind the wheel. Nigel moved to let Mrs. Kennedy sit beside the driver and listened with equal interest as everything was explained; one never knew, Jean might forget and he would remember. Five minutes later, feeling confident because the woman beside her gave her that feeling, Jean drove away from the house. At first she moved slowly and cautiously,

118

as this car responded so swiftly to each touch of her hands and feet whereas with the other she had had to struggle with the gears and brakes.

Alone in the back seat Marie nursed the tennis racquets and watched the back of her daughter's head with great pride. Jean was so quick to learn anything and the ability to drive was a necessity when one lived so far from a town. Then she began to wonder what she could buy her girl for her twenty-first birthday in another month's time.

"Feeling all right?" asked Mrs. Kennedy, and Jean flashed her a smile of gratitude and thanks. "Good! We'll stop at the police station to get a learner's permit – I do believe in keeping the law even if we live in the Never-Never, then you'll have nothing to fear from anyone."

She leaned back in her seat, her placid glance resting on the road ahead, a road she had travelled over so many times, doing nothing to distract her pupil's attention. Beside her Nigel kept up one of his running commentaries which she found rather interesting and illuminating and she chuckled to herself as the boy, in a low voice because he thought his mother might be listening, went on to explain that though this was the kind of car he would like they would have to put up with what they had because Uncle could not afford anything better.

"I shouldn't tell everyone that," she answered in a low grave voice. "Uncle might not like it. He can't help being poor."

"No." Nigel sighed. "I feel sorry for him, because he's so nice and he gives you plenty of what he has. I like the oranges out here –" his voice droned on and on.

Jean felt like singing. There was no expressionless voice telling her what or what not to do, no unfriendly eyes watching her every movement and if she made a mistake as she did once or twice at the beginning of that trip into town, no exaggerated sighs or frowns to shake her confidence. Under Mrs. Kennedy's instructions she turned off the main road and stopped outside the police station, a house which possessed a gay and colourful front garden and many shady trees, and went inside to return within a very few minutes waving a piece of paper and with large L-plates.

"Now we're quite respectable," cried Mrs. Kennedy. "And seeing the tennis courts are just down here we won't bother with the L's just now."

Marie and Nigel left them there to search for a barbers and wander through the shops. The town was quiet and still. There was a sleepy atmosphere about it as very little traffic moved along the red gravel road during the early afternoon. Two large semi-trailers each with a load of sheep passed them as they waited under the shade of the jacaranda trees and from the direction of the station came the sound of shunting trucks. But even they sounded leisurely.

"It isn't a very big place, is it?" asked Jean, who was looking round with great curiosity.

"We've a population of about two thousand. It's a very rich area – the land, I mean, not the people," said Anne Kennedy, quickly thinking of Nigel's remarks.

Jean picked her up quickly. "If the land is rich why not the people?"

"Some of them are. A great deal depends upon climatic conditions and the way a man works on the land; a good year means good crops, drought can mean the ruination of hopes for a long time."

"That's what Uncle said," answered Jean thoughtfully. She had learnt a great deal during the time she had spent on the property, for she had kept her eyes and her ears open. "I understand there hasn't been a real drought up here for a long time."

Mrs. Kennedy looked at her. "We've had good seasons," she admitted, then added briskly, "I think we'd better be

120

going, Jean, it's nearly three o'clock and Valerie will be waiting."

The girl hesitated for a moment as though loath to drop this discussion of the land, then a smile lit her face and she moved away from the kerb, wishing Rob would be at the courts when she arrived. Dearly she would have liked to have seen the expression on his face when she pulled up in state driving this large well-kept car. But Valerie's face was equally expressive, and for a moment she gaped at the sight of Jean casually reaching over into the back seat for her racquets and then stepping out, a trim little figure in her white blouse and shorts, her tanned legs bare and with white socks and sand-shoes on her small feet.

I wish I didn't feel such a schoolgirl in this get-up, thought Jean, then she heard her companion saying blandly:

"Here we are. Jean has driven me for a change. She says it's so nice to drive a decent car instead of those old things they have at Peppertree Lane." And Mrs. Kennedy was very busy pushing the two tell-tale plates out of sight as she spoke.

As she moved on to the courts and was introduced to the other players Jean knew that in Anne Kennedy she had met someone who understood her and who would be a friend. Indeed, no matter how long she stayed at Peppertree Lane or whatever happened there.

CHAPTER TEN

As far as Jean was concerned it was a highly successful afternoon. The sky was clouded over and consequently there was no glare and it was cool. She had not played for a long time and as often happens she played better for having had a respite. She was and always had been very much at home on a tennis court; being small and agile she could dart here, there and everywhere with little effort, and though her arm was short it had plenty of strength and her services and returns were of a high standard. More than once she saw Valerie bite her lips and could not help a glow of satisfaction because she was the better player of the two. Valerie might ride, play golf and do many other things she could not do herself, but on a tennis court there was no comparison between them. Mrs. Kennedy was quick to notice that after the first two sets Valerie did not play against Jean again.

A dainty afternoon tea was served in the small pavilion. Jean had not known each player was supposed to bring something and wished she could have produced one of her mother's fluffy sponges or juicy fruit cakes, but her companion produced a small basket which held enough food for a small picnic by itself and told her not to worry. There would be other occasions when Mrs. Delaney's baking could be chewed on and criticised. Conversation drifted, as it had done the night of the dinner at Valerie's home, from one subject to another, and Jean listened again to the local gossip and bit thoughtfully into a curried egg sandwich, for which she had a great weakness, when one lady laughingly told them she had been given a fur coat as a gift from her husband when he had received his wool cheque. Jean had no desire for a fur coat; in any case it was doubtful if she would wear it in this climate, for there were no biting cold winds such as they had often had in Melbourne, no stinging rain blowing in from the sea and few cloudy days such as they were enjoying today. Since their arrival there had been nothing but warm sunny days. All she wanted was the material for the loose covers for the suite in the lounge, some new curtains and knick-knacks in the bedrooms, new bedspreads and rugs and more paint so that she could tackle the outside of Peppertree Lane. Perhaps Uncle Gerald also received a wool cheque? He had plenty of sheep.

"When is Pop coming home again?" asked Valerie at her elbow, and she started.

"We have no idea," Jean confessed. "A telegram was phoned through yesterday to say he wouldn't be arriving on Wednesday, that was all there was to it." She laughed and the other girl smiled.

"He doesn't waste words, does he?"

"He doesn't waste anything," remarked one of the others dryly.

"I want to see him." Valerie looked thoughtful. She said she wanted to arrange about the barbecue he had mentioned; it would be fun sitting round a huge fire with steak and chops grilling over the embers. It was a long time since anyone had had a barbecue and she could not imagine either Jean or Mrs. Delaney having attended such things before. Even if they had it had been in a city – and there was a difference, she thought rather superciliously.

Anne Kennedy got to her feet and reached for her racquet. "Let's have another game and then we must go. We have further to drive than anyone else."

"How far are you out from town?" asked Jean curiously as they walked on to the court.

"Thirty-two miles."

"And don't you ever feel lonely?"

"Gracious, no! I've too much to do with my time.

There's a large garden and now I attend to it myself. We had an old gardener, but he died a few months ago." Her face clouded over a moment and Jean received the impression that she had had a soft spot for the gardener. "I make all my preserves and bottle such quantities of fruit, and there's much planning and thought necessary with a large property. I help my husband all I can. Then I have to look after him, of course!"

"You make that sound such a pleasure!" Jean smiled. "I'm looking forward so much to going there tonight."

"Once you have the legal use of the car," Mrs. Kennedy's voice was lowered discreetly, "you can come any time you wish, my dear, and you'll always be welcome."

Marie and Nigel were waiting in town, the latter attired like a Red Indian, and rather defiantly her mother faced Jean when she surveyed her brother's magnificence with raised eyebrows.

"I bought it for him as something extra to play with," she said in a firm voice. "He gets lonely out there in the daytime and now he can pretend he's prowling over the prairies. It's easier to pretend when you have the right clothes and things to pretend with!"

"Popski and I are going on the trail tomorrow." Nigel lifted a bow and arrow and put it down hurriedly when he saw the look on his mother's face. He *had* promised not to use it in town – that was the only condition he had been allowed to wear the feathers in his hair and the gaily decorated sackcloth shirt and trousers. He spent the time shooting imaginary arrows out of the car windows during the long drive out to Gum Valley and firmly claimed a bag of at least three horses and ten sheep, as well as a few wild ducks and some galahs. The big car, still being driven by Jean who was much more confident and at home behind the wheel this time, reached the other homestead in the brief time between sunset and darkness and there Mrs. Kennedy alighted and led the way indoors.

Jean looked round with interest. It was very hard to believe that this house, tucked away between trees on the river bank, was so far from any other habitation. The rooms were as large as those at Peppertree Lane, and there was some of the same type of heavy furniture, but there the resemblance ended. Each room was thickly carpeted, there were comfortable-looking cushions in all the chairs, flowers were everywhere and electric lights gleamed softly from behind modern fittings on all the walls. The bathroom was a revelation; even in Melbourne she had seen nothing like it, and as she had a wash in clear hot water, brushed her hair and powdered her nose again she felt as though she should pinch herself to make sure she really was thirty-two miles from even Murra Creek. That western township did not impress either Jean or her mother very much.

As Jean changed into something more suitable for dinner than her tennis clothes and which she had brought with her in a small suitcase, she thought the same thing. This home was luxurious and very comfortable and pensively she gazed around at the glorious carpet, the pretty contrasting bedspreads and curtains and the little odds and ends placed only for the convenience of guests, and she sighed. Wealth did not shout at you, but everything was just right for where it was and what it was there for; it all looked used, lived in and loved. Very much different from Mrs. Miller's home – the only other one Jean had visited in the district – and from the house which they now called home. But that was improving steadily, she thought staunchly, and as the months went by and her mother saved a little each time from her housekeeping allowance more and more improvements would be made.

Nigel was in the garden stalking a cat with her four kittens in the half light. He only pretended to shoot them with the arrows, for he was looking with great yearning at the smallest kitten and wondering how he could work the conversation round to the subject of cats during dinner. He

125

could say he hadn't a kitten and would like one very much. If he said it innocently enough perhaps Mrs. Kennedy would take pity on him and give him one. His mother would soon have something to say if he asked outright.

"And what do you think you're doing?" asked a voice from away above him, and the boy raised his head with a startled gesture.

"Oh, you frightened me! I'm stalking cats," he admitted, the angelic look on his face very pronounced. "Gee, you're tall! Taller than Rob."

The man who was looking down at him laughed and pointed to the bow and arrows.

"Kill anything?"

"No." Nigel looked horrified. "I wouldn't really shoot kittens, they're lovely little things, aren't they?" and added hopefully, "Have you many?"

"Too many. Surely you have cats and their offspring out at Peppertree Lane?"

"Oh yes, but they're mostly wild ones," said the boy regretfully as he got to his feet. "You know, they won't let you stroke them, and I like stroking kittens, don't you?"

"No, I do not!"

Nigel looked up at him. "You're Mr. Kennedy?" The man nodded. "I thought you must be. Rob once said that you were the most truthful man he'd ever met and that you never pulled any punches, whatever that means."

Pat Kennedy flung back his head and his laughter reached the three women who were waiting for him in the lounge. Jean lifted her head. Nigel again! This time the laughter would not die out of the man's eyes as he came into the house and she waited, curiously intent, as the footsteps resounded along the veranda and the french windows were opened to allow Nigel and their host to enter. She sighed; the laughter was still there, in his whole expression, and it did not fade as his wife made the introductions and he shook Marie's hand first and then her own.

126

"Mrs. Delaney and her daughter Jean. This is my husband."

Jean had to raise her head to look at him and she smiled. "You're another one who towers above me!" she exclaimed.

"I see you've already met Nigel," laughed Mrs. Kennedy, nodding towards the boy.

"Yes." He rumpled the boy's hair, disarranging the circle of feathers. "He was stalking kittens out on the lawn."

"We haven't any at home," said Nigel rather pathetically, refusing to look at either his sister or his mother. "Not tame ones anyway."

"You can have a couple if you like. I shall be glad to get rid of them." Anne was watching him and knew she had said the very thing he had intended her to say, and her lips twitched. "Remind me to get them before you leave."

"Oh, thank you!" he cried rapturously, and did not mind when his mother hustled him hurriedly away to have a wash. He had gained his wish and had witnesses to prove he had done it fairly.

Marie said later that it was one of the most enjoyable evenings she had ever spent in anyone's home; the atmosphere was warm and friendly, the conversation light and enjoyable, and after Nigel had fallen asleep in a chair she and Jean played cards with their host and hostess. Jean wondered what Rob was doing and if he had been annoyed because there had been no meal ready upon his return home. Perhaps he was taking it out on the poor piano at this very moment.

"Penny for them," offered her host, looking at her with one eyebrow raised, and she realised that everyone was waiting for her to play her card. Guiltily she looked down at her hand, a slow flush creeping over her cheeks, and Marie began to wonder if chasing about the court during the afternoon had given Jean a chill and that was a tem-

127

perature she was getting.

Jean was quite content to be driven home at nearly midnight. She had done enough for one day and was sleepy. She had her permit and as soon as her uncle returned she would ask his permission to use the utility whenever it was not needed elsewhere. Sitting in the front seat, Nigel was curled up in his mother's arm at the back with two bewildered kittens hugged to him. She watched, in the light of the dashboard, the steady brown hands of the man beside her, still storing up information for use in the future and hardly able to believe she had brought this big car out from town only a few hours previously over this bumpy track. She thought of a remark passed by Mrs. Kennedy as they were preparing to leave. She had mentioned that she was playing golf the following weekend and Jean had immediately said she couldn't play but hoped that one day she would be able to do so.

"It's not necessary, you know," said the other woman gently, "to do all these things. If I were you, Jean, I should stay on the tennis court – you have few equals."

It was sensible advice, thought Jean drowsily. She could play tennis and maybe it would be years before she attained the same proficiency on the golf course. Anyway, she had not the money at present to purchase the necessary irons required and until she and her mother had purchased those loose covers it would be better to forget the idea altogether.

Rather timidly, because she did not wish to sound too forward, Marie had extended an invitation to Mr. and Mrs. Kennedy to have dinner and spend an evening at Peppertree Lane in about a fortnight's time. This had been accepted promptly and with thanks and she hoped Gerald would not mind having visitors – but why should he? she reasoned; they were people he knew well and he would not have the preparations beforehand. What a difference it would make to the lounge if she could buy the material for those loose covers before then! She brooded over ways and means of coaxing a few pounds out of her brother-in-law within the next few days.

When they returned Rob came out of the house, obviously intending to have a word with whoever had brought the women home.

"Hullo, Rob." Pat Kennedy greeted him and he stood back as his friend came into the hall with Nigel in his arms. The child was still clutching the kittens in his sleep and Jean saw Rob smile when he saw them peeping out of the boy's coat. Marie led the way to his bedroom, while Jean remained on the veranda to confront an angry and somewhat puzzled Rob.

"So that's where you've been?" he demanded.

"Is there anything wrong in accepting an invitation to dinner?"

"You might have told me you were going and that I was supposed to find my own meal."

"You never asked! You might have remembered I'd been invited to play tennis and inquired how I was going to get there."

"I'd forgotten."

"That's a poor excuse. Sam was supposed to give you dinner –"

"I wasn't going searching for it!"

There was a significant cough behind them and Jean and Rob spun round.

"Mr. Kennedy, thank you so much for a very enjoyable evening and also for bringing us home."

She knew that her cheeks were red and that Rob looked as though he wanted a very small excuse to burst forth into one of his tempers.

"It's all been a great pleasure," Pat Kennedy assured her, smiling. "And both Anne and myself will be looking forward to coming here soon. I enjoy evenings with Pop too, his conversation is always so illuminating!" He turned to Rob. "I see improvements here, Robby boy – you must have been busy."

Rob hesitated and then gave the credit where it was due, although Jean was sure that it was much against his will.

"This is principally her doing." He waved his hand towards the girl and she bit her lip. Couldn't he call her Jean? How much better it would have sounded!

Pat looked from his face to the girl's, smiled again and said he must be driving back, his wife would still be waiting for him. As soon as the gate shut behind him Rob turned on his heel, went to his room and slammed the door.

"I don't think he had any dinner!" said Marie wonderingly, coming from Nigel's room with the kittens in her hands. "I've just peeped into the kitchen and there isn't a thing out of place. If Sam had brought something over or if he'd made anything himself I'm sure there would have been *some* mess left for us to clear up! Now where do I put these cats?"

Pop arrived by plane from Sydney early on Friday morning and managed to get a lift from the airfield to Murra Creek. There he dawdled about the streets for an hour or so, meeting his friends, calling in at this office or that shop and savouring the sun on his face again. It had been raining when he left Sydney. Finally he hired a taxi to take him home and collected a number of parcels from the station, these had come ahead of him by train, and he then sat back to think over what he had been doing.

The investments had been handled satisfactorily. They had been the first and most important things he had attended to when he reached the city. And as that was the principal, indeed the only reason why he had travelled three hundred miles, he felt content and proceeded to wander through the large stores on the second day in search of the pans Marie wanted without any of the usual qualms he felt in such places. In the hardware department he looked round with amazement; never had he seen so many kitchen utensils in all his life, and he scratched his head as he surveyed the pyramids of gleaming aluminium and enamel. If one of each of these things were necessary in a kitchen, how on earth did Marie and Jean manage with what they had at Peppertree Lane?

A young girl came towards him and inquired if there was anything he needed. Pop thrust the newspaper cutting into her hand and said:

"Pans. Like those."

"How many?"

"All of 'em."

"You mean the set? There are six together, various sizes. These are the ones." She led the way towards another pile of shining pans and held out the set, one inside the other.

"They'll do. Send 'em to this address." He wrote it on the edge of the paper.

That had been easy, the easiest order his sister-in-law could have given him, and he could now walk out of the shop feeling he had done his duty. But he hesitated as he gazed round and beckoned the girl to return to his side.

"Wait. I'll have something else. Gadgets!" There were plenty of gadgets for use in a kitchen – egg-beaters, strainers, fancy tin-openers, there was something no matter where he looked. He thrust some notes into the girl's hand. "Give me gadgets for that amount."

She stared at him and at the notes in her hand. Obviously he came from the country; no city-dweller even in this climate had that ruddy colour which was the result of living an outdoor life. Perhaps he was a grazier and had a daughter who was getting married shortly and who would need these things in her new home. The assistant had rather hazy ideas as to what could or could not be purchased in the country.

Satisfied at last with the pile of gadgets, which would surely delight the two at home, Pop wandered off and eventually found himself, whether by accident or design – he

131

refused to argue with his conscience as to which it was – in the toy department. Looking round, he drew a deep breath and felt suddenly like a benevolent Santa Claus. Not only Nigel was going to have toys, there were others in Murra Creek who deserved them for the only, and to his mind the very simple reason, that they were children.

Another girl came towards him and he looked at her beneath his thick white bushy eyebrows and she eyed him hesitatingly and meeting the twinkle in his eyes she smiled in reply. Rob explained that he needed lots and lots of toys and some had to be sent to addresses which he would give her as he chose the things. He warned her he would probably be here a long time and if she found that thought too much for her she could send for someone else to serve him. The girl shook her head definitely and for the next two hours they stayed together, she explaining how some toys worked, he playing with them all and trying them out on the floor. Not since Rob had been a boy had he enjoyed himself so much and when he was finally satisfied he made another of the impulsive gestures which he so liked doing, he pressed a few notes into her hand, patted her cheek in a grandfatherly manner and told her to buy a toy for herself.

Jean. He could not return without a gift for her, and the bushy eyebrows met as he tried to think of something she would like. It had not to be expensive, not too expensive anyway. Clothes? He shook his head definitely. For one thing he did not know her size and for another, he would not go into one of the ladies' departments to please his niece or anyone else. Books? He had little idea of her tastes. Something for her own room? He tried to think of the bedroom Jean now owned. There was little in it, if he remembered rightly. He did not know, though, if there was a double or a single bed in there. His brow cleared as he recollected something she had said one evening as she sat near him on the veranda, mending some socks of Rob's.

"I'll have to get something to keep my belongings together. I've mending wool in one box, sewing cottons in another –"

One of those workbasket things – he thought he had seen one somewhere, it stood on legs and the top closed down to form a small table. So he strode off in a different direction, and it was only after he had paid for the latest and neatest of workbaskets did he remember he was supposed to have little money and should not be frittering it away on such fancy things.

Ah well. He went down the stairs, mistrusting both the lift and the escalator. I must have sold some sheep while I've been down here. Must have sold something. And Rob – he'll have something to say about it too! Must buy him something. Bless the boy! Now let me think, what hasn't he got?

And the very newest of fishing rods was added to his collection.

Now he was nearly home, most of the precious parts beside him or on the back seat. As the taxi turned into the lane of peppers the smile faded from his face and he surveyed the house which grew nearer each moment with a look of uneasiness in his eyes. It looked very different from what it had done before he went away; what had been happening here in his absence? Then he realised what it was and nodded when the taxi driver, who had also been staring, pulled up beside the gate and grinned.

"Someone's been busy, Pop!"

"Someone has." And he knew who it was too, he thought, stepping to the ground and marching up and down the fence. The lantana bushes were bare and tidy and they would come again, cutting them back would improve them; the peppers, shorn of their lower greenery, cleared the top of the fence for the first time in years and the green gate which had always squeaked and which had caused the friction between his niece and his foster-son seemed to beckon him up a path which had been cleared of weeds on either

133

side. Pop looked at it all with his head on one side.

"Well, well!" he murmured. "What a girl!"

The parcels were carefully placed on the veranda, he nodded to his driver, flung his hat on a chair, poked the cattle-dog with the toe of his shoe as she waved a welcoming tail without bothering to get up and crept indoors. Jean must be out somewhere, for the kitchen was empty – Pop came to an abrupt halt in the kitchen door.

Red and white check gingham hung on either side of the long window, red paint, just touches of it showed up well against the cream enamel on the cupboards and doors. There was a red geranium in a brown pot in the centre of the large kitchen table which had been scrubbed white and on the gleaming fireplace a copper kettle bubbled at him cheerfully.

"Oh, blimey!" he whispered wonderingly, and looked at the floor. That definitely spoilt the whole effect. The bare concrete should not be showing; it reminded him too much of the milking shed, and something would have to be done about it.

In the dining-room he drew in his breath again. Elizabeth used to have long graceful curtains such as these in her dining-room; why had he not realised before how bare and uncomfortable was this home of his? It had needed a woman's touch, for no man would ever think of placing a huge vaseful of pink and white chrysanthemums in that dark corner, or of arranging the silver bowl on the sideboard without them appearing too stiff and formal, or of washing a rug. Pop crept over to the fireplace the better to admire the large sheepskin spread before it and he stood there with his back to the grate which had had its bareness covered with sprays from the passion vine in another silver bowl and with his hands in his pockets surveyed everything critically again. It looked good and he liked it. Then he smiled. How much had Marie spent on the curtains in here and in the kitchen? It would be interesting to know. Also

134

HAVE YOU MISSED ANY OF THESE MILLS & BOON ROMANCES?

ALL PRICED AT 20p SEE OVER FOR HANDY ORDER FORM PLEASE TICK YOUR REQUIREMENTS

FREE!

YOUR COPY OF OUR MAGAZINE OF
MILLS & BOON ROMANCES NOW
AVAILABLE ON REQUEST

Over the page are listed 50 selections from our current
catalogue. Why not contact your local stockist to obtain
these books? However, should you have any difficulty please
write to us at MILLS & BOON READER SERVICE,
P.O. BOX 236, 14 Sanderstead Road, S. Croydon, Surrey,
CR2 0YG, England, ticking the titles you require, and en-
closing your remittance. All Mills & Boon paperbacks
ordered through the Reader Service are 20p. Please note to
cover postage and handling, will United Kingdom readers
add 2p per book. Overseas readers are asked to add 10p per
book and use International Money Orders where possible.

Please send me the free Mills & Boon Romance magazine   ☐

Please send me the titles ticked   ☐

I enclose £.. (No C.O.D.)

Name .... Miss/Mrs

Address ....

Town/City ....

County/Country.......................... Postal/Zip Code...............

MB3/74

where she had got the money from. Also what Rob had to say about it. The old man's shoulders shook with mirth as he silently went through the rest of the house and then returned to the veranda, where he picked up the parcels and took them with him into his bedroom and after changing he hurried outside, anxious to breathe into his lungs this warm dry air and to look again at the land that was his.

CHAPTER ELEVEN

JEAN spent the morning out in the paddocks with Jack, the mechanic. He had told her during the course of conversation, when she called into the shed for a screwdriver, that he was driving out there with the morning smoke-oh for the men and asked in a tentative kind of way if she would like to go with him. The girl looked at him thoughtfully for a moment or two, then she inquired if Rob would be there too and upon being informed that he would not she promptly accepted the invitation. In a fit of mischief she fetched the large L-plates from her bedroom, fastened them on very securely in a prominent position with pieces of wire and sat demurely behind the driving wheel of the old bomb with Scruffy perched up beside her and waited for Jack. When he came out with the basket containing the food for the men's morning break he looked, smiled and calmly took his seat beside her. "Mr. Rob, he told me you hadn't to touch the utility, but he didn't mention this, Miss Jean," he remarked.

"I was a very wicked girl, because I took the ute out by myself last weekend without asking permission," she confessed, driving down the track.

"So he said." Jack grinned. That was not all Mr. Rob had said to him. "You've learnt pretty quickly, I must say."

"Mrs. Kennedy let me drive her car on Wednesday – it was much easier to handle than this, and so much more comfortable!"

He eyed her with respect. If Mrs. Kennedy could trust this slip of a thing with her large expensive car why did Mr. Rob create such a fuss about her driving round in something which should have been sold to the scrap dealers years ago? There was no danger, no traffic, and Miss Jean did not strike him as being the kind of girl who would scream or cover her eyes with her hands in a sudden emergency. Look at the way she stopped by the gate, quietly and without fuss!

"I haven't gone backwards yet," announced Miss Jean after he had opened it and she had driven through and waited until he regained his seat.

"That's easy." Jack glanced at the massive old watch on his left wrist. "We're in plenty of time, we'll have a bit of practice. Drive down into the next paddock, they've ploughed in here and won't thank us for chasing about all over it – now stop here. O.K. That's the gear that puts you in reverse –"

He was helpful and kind and knew the old car inside out. Jean learnt more in the half hour with him as her instructor than she had done during the whole afternoon when by herself, for he explained how things worked and why and obviously enjoyed doing it. Finally he made her drive in reverse through the open gates, not once but many times until he was satisfied, then they continued on their way to where the trio were waiting by the side of one of the huge paddocks with two tractors and a truck, the former with combines behind them and the latter laden with drums of fuel, oil and water.

"It's a pity you have only this old thing out here to drive," she said.

"Mr. Rob had a nice car, but just before you came it vanished for some reason or another." Jack had often wished he dared to ask where the red convertible had gone, but when he did remember it, it would be just one of those occasions when Mr. Rob came into the machinery shed and looked round with a frown and that tightness round his mouth which always appeared when something went wrong. And all of them had learnt from experience that to speak out of place then was inviting trouble.

Jean looked only slightly interested. "Did he? What kind was it?"

"One of those low coupé affairs – you know, open most of the time. Lovely bus it was too, and could he speed into Murra Creek! Said he held the unofficial record! Very dashing he looked in it too!" The old bomb screeched to a halt and he clicked his tongue. "That was bad, Miss Jean!"

"I'm sorry."

He glanced at her face. She looked rather tight-lipped as well, but he thought that was perhaps because she felt she had shown up her ignorance in front of the other men who were now crowding round eager for their tucker and the break in the monotonous hours of rumbling backwards and forwards across the paddock.

A fire had already been lit and the billy was boiling, another tin mug had been added after her arrival and a log was pushed over for her to sit on. Jean shared the contents of the basket and grimaced a little at the strength and blackness of the tea when it was handed to her. Marvelling again at a large expanse of land round her, she listened as they discussed the prospects of rain and as Mr. Rob had said it would do so before the weekend they knew it would, especially as he had ordered them to start with the sowing of oats and barley. He was rarely wrong about the weather. Perhaps, suggested Ben, it was because he had been born out here, and he had made a careful study of clouds and their formations, wind, rainfall registrations and aboriginal beliefs and superstitions.

"And *they* know what they're talking about too, some of the old darkies. Look at Mike. That's the chap who attended to your dog, Miss Jean." He nodded in the direction taken by the nondescript-looking dog who was chasing smells and imaginary rabbits. "He can tell you all sorts of things when he wants, stories handed down through the ages of floods, fires and droughts."

138

"This climate isn't what it used to be," remarked Jack rather sadly, eyeing one of Sam's currant biscuits with suspicion.

"Mike always remind me of a feller I knew in Charleville," began Bruce, and promptly launched into a long account of all this man had told him of the weather in the past. Jean felt guilty; they were obviously entertaining her and forgetting their work. If Rob appeared on the scene unexpectedly they would all catch the brunt of his annoyance. So she scrambled to her feet to pick up the collection of mugs and they took the hint, stretched and flung the ends of their cigarettes into the brown soil. Naurally they wanted to show her the combines and explain how they worked. Ben offered to take her round the paddock and she went with him, finding conversation was well-nigh impossible over the roar of the tractor as it pulled the massive machinery. She was soon covered in red dust and had oily streaks down one leg and on her dress before she alighted again. Ben waved farewell and she lingered with Jack watching them at work, occasionally glancing at the overcast sky and wishing it would rain.

Jean pulled up in front of the machinery shed at the same moment as Rob drove up the track from the opposite direction in the utility, and through the windscreen they looked at each other warily. Jack, after glancing at the young boss's face, slid quietly from his seat and disappeared, knowing quite well he would hear more of this later. A pity, he thought, that Mr. Rob did not like Miss Jean. The girl switched off the engine as Rob got slowly to the ground and stiffened as he came towards her.

"Well?" he asked in a cold biting voice, and she resisted the great temptation to answer as Nigel might have done: "I'm quite well, thanks!"

"Didn't I tell you not to do this again?" he asked sharply. "Where's Jack? I'll have his hide for disobeying my orders —"

"I asked him," she interrupted, determined to defend the mechanic, he at least had been kind and understanding about her wish to drive and had found no fault in the idea. "So you can leave him out of it altogether. The fault, if there is one, is mine."

"What's the meaning of all this palaver?" He waved his hand towards the L-plates.

"They're necessary when you have a permit, aren't they?"

"Permit? When and where did you get that?"

"From the police station at Murra Creek on Wednesday," she answered in detail. "I drove there in Mrs. Kennedy's car –"

"*You* drove – in her car?" he asked incredulously.

"And why not? She asked me if I would like to, so naturally I said yes. Not everyone in this part of the world is as stuffy as you!"

A tremor crossed Rob's brown face. "Whatever she's foolish enough to do, or let you do, you aren't going to do it here! Don't touch either this or the utility again –"

"You make me feel furious!" cried Jean, feeling suddenly very angry and conscious of her appearance, so windblown and dust-covered, and she had a momentary thought of a convertible which had been removed from sight, for some reason or another, before the arrival of the Delaneys. The colour in her cheeks deepened with indignation. "I'm doing no wrong, yet you persist in carrying on in this babyish and mulish manner, and will give me no definite reason why I shouldn't drive everything there is on the place! It's not yours!" She faced him defiantly. "You aren't the owner here and I refuse to take any more orders from you, do you understand?"

"I'm in charge of these vehicles," insisted Rob. "So it's no use refusing to obey any orders I give in here –"

"It's no concern of yours what I drive or try to drive. I won't be dictated to! You've been against all we've done since the first day we arrived here, and both Mother and myself are tired of it. It's the same in the house –"

"Yes, in the house too!" Rob let his tongue run away with him. He flew into one of his sudden furies. "I've lived here for years with Pop and we've been happy on our own, then you come along and alter everything! It's all different from what it was and I'm not going to stand on one side and watch you spoil everything we've treasured. You're nothing but a little gold-digger –"

"How dare you, a jackaroo, speak to me like this!" she asked in a strangled voice.

"I'll talk to you how I like! Now get down from there and get out of my sight before I say something really rude! Get down!"

Jean sat down and clutched the driving wheel firmly with both hands. "I won't," she said flatly. "I won't do as you tell me, especially when you speak to me like you have been doing –"

"Oh, yes, you will!" He moved towards her and before she could speak his arms reached out and she was lifted bodily from her seat.

"Put me down!" she commanded fiercely, her heart pounding and looking straight into his eyes. Then her hand came up and caught his cheek. Rob swore softly and swung away from the car taking her with him, and Scruffy, who had been watching with his head on one side, began to realise that someone was handling his beloved mistress in a manner she did not like and which was not usual, and flew to her defence. The hair on the back of his neck rose stiffly, he bared his teeth and was out of the door in a flash, catching Rob's wrist between his jaws. In the sudden pain at this unexpected attack Rob immediately dropped his burden and Jean stumbled to her feet, swinging round to stop him landing out with his foot at the dog who was watching and waiting for the next move.

"Don't touch him," she said very quietly, her fingers

gripping his arm tightly.

They stared at each other. Jean was trembling and her hair fell in disorder over her hot forehead. Rob was white with temper and was grasping his right wrist with his left hand; blood was already dripping between his fingers. She felt him relax a little and Scruffy moved nearer to her side, still wary and uncertain, determined to fight to the death in her defence if necessary. Jean looked down at a drop of blood fell on her bare arm.

"You'd better attend to that immediately, Rob," she said softly, and without another word he turned towards the house and she watched him go, her slight figure drooping a little. Then she whirled round on the dog.

"Why did you do that?" she asked passionately. "You naughty, horrid dog! You shouldn't have bitten him, you shouldn't have touched him! No, don't crawl round me like that. I'm very annoyed with you, and now *you* can get out of my sight!"

Jean received a shock when Pop sauntered casually into the kitchen to inquire if lunch was ready as he was extremely hungry.

"Whenever did you arrive?" Marie was flustered by his appearance and glanced round, wondering if he had had time to notice all they had been doing.

"Short time ago." He sniffed. "Something smells good!"

"Cornish pasties. Made with mutton, of course."

"Ah!" Then he did look towards the windows. "Been busy, Marie?"

"We've been busy everywhere. Do you – do you think it looks any better, Gerald?"

"Yes," he answered bluntly, walking round the table and touching the cupboard doors. "Where did you get the paint?"

"From Rob. After a lot of argument – he was very much against the idea, I'm afraid. But I told him that if I was to spend the greater part of my time in here I must make it presentable, it was too dark and dingy before." She paused. "We've been making alterations in the other rooms, too, Gerald. I hope you don't mind."

"Why should I?"

"Come and look." Leading the way into the dining-room she waved her hands around in an absent manner.

"Nice curtains," he remarked as though this was the first time he had seen them. "Where did you get 'em?"

"Jean and I made them." She darted a glance at his face. "From some tablecloths we discovered in an old suitcase. You must have forgotten them and I thought you wouldn't mind if I used them in this manner. They cost nothing but the few cents for the dye," she added hastily.

"Oh!" That surprised him and he smiled a little behind his hand. Enterprising women! Used their brains. "I would never have thought it possible to make curtains from table-cloths. They must have been Elizabeth's, for I never bought so many or such large ones."

Marie was agitated, her hands would not stay still, in fact she looked as though she was still wringing out a dish-cloth or something and she kept looking anxiously at him.

"It's started to rain," he said, refusing to help her in any way.

"That will be nice for you, especially as they've started sowing." He raised his eyebrows at that remark. "Gerald —" Still she hesitated and he went on looking at her, wondering what all this was about and wishing she would get on with it whatever it was. Hesitation annoyed him. "I've something to tell you. About Jean." Her daughter opened her mouth ready to explain, but Marie silenced her. "I'm sure she has every intention of telling you herself, but I consider it my duty to explain, for she did it with my full approval and I don't think you should be annoyed with her. It caused a little trouble with the jackaroo — he does seem to consider he's somebody out here and personally I think

143

he takes too much on himself —"

"Get on with it," he cried testily.

"She's been learning to drive," she said breathlessly, and waited.

"Well?"

Jean looked at him. He did not seem at all perturbed about the idea, in fact she was sure there was a twinkle in the eyes half hidden by those bushy white eyebrows.

"Don't you mind?"

"It's a good idea."

"Oh!" She thought for a moment. "I'm glad you've said that, for Rob has been most unpleasant about it —"

"So I believe," he murmured to himself.

"And it's so silly, for she picked up the whole idea very quickly — she's a capable child, you know. Capable enough, anyway, for Mrs. Kennedy to let her drive her car," Marie said.

"Who taught her?"

"Nigel in the first place," she answered warily. "He didn't actually drive, of course, but he knew what to do and explained it to his sister." She smiled at him. "I'm so glad you don't mind, Gerald. I'd like to learn myself," she went on frankly. "It would be so useful to be able to go into town whenever Nigel needs a haircut, for instance, as he did the other day. Or whenever I wanted to visit friends or go shopping. We were at the Kennedys' one evening for dinner, after Jean had been playing tennis with Valerie, and I've asked them here for an evening shortly. Is that all right with you?"

Pop smiled. "Sure. It's as much your home now as mine. Where's the boy?" he finished.

Marie shrugged her shoulders helplessly. "I don't know. As soon as the morning's lessons are over he vanishes until his stomach, by some method I've never been able to discover, informs him that the meal is ready."

He chuckled and Jean and her mother left the room

happy that the confession had been made and that Gerald did not object to anything that had been done in his absence. Marie had not expected him to enthuse. Men didn't, she knew that from experience, it was either all right or it wasn't, and if it wasn't you did it again until it was.

Gerald smiled as he watched her go. His sister-in-law looked and sounded quite contented, and if it was the curtains that had made her so she had better find some more bits of material. He wanted to keep Nigel here. But before he went looking for the boy he must have a few words with Rob and explain that he did not like caveman tactics.

His foster-son was where he had expected to find him, in his own room, and his moody eyes changed their expression immediately the door opened and he saw who was here.

"Pop!" There was gladness and thankfulness in his voice, it was so good to have the old chap safe home again. "Hello, Pop!"

"Hello, son." They merely looked at each other for a moment, content to be together again.

"When did you get in? I didn't hear you arrive."

"This morning's plane, lift to Murra Creek, taxi home. What happened?"

Pop pointed to the awkward-looking bandage which had been tied round his wrist, and Rob lowered his eyes and turned away to sit down on the chair near the window, pushing from it a couple of books and his tennis racquet.

"I was bitten," he muttered, his anger mounting again as he remembered what had bitten him and why.

"Spider?" asked Pop with interest.

"No. A dog."

The other man clicked his tongue. "Which dog? Can't have that going on round here." He looked towards the rifle propped up in a corner and Rob, following the direction of his eyes, flinched a little. Imagine what would happen if that small spitfire discovered her dog was to be shot! "Your face too, son. Been bitten there as well?"

145

Rob's hand went to cover the red mark left by those stinging little fingers and the skin around it became nearly the same colour as he flushed. "No."

"Very reticent about it, aren't you?" asked Pop, watching him and wondering how he would explain the bite away.

"It was nothing," said Rob, and tried to change the subject. "How did you get on in Sydney? Were the investments in order?" Pop nodded. "And what delayed you?"

"Gadgets. Lose your temper with the dog?"

"No!"

They glared at each other across the room. It was not the first time they had clashed and Rob turned away when he saw the look on the other man's face. He wanted an explanation and he would get it.

"Explain!" commanded Pop curtly.

"Oh, it was her dog –" Rob nodded towards the great outdoors. "He bit me."

"Why?"

"Because – because I lost my temper, if you must know. Pop, there've been such goings-on here while you've been away –"

"You're quite right!" Pop walked across the room. "I've seen 'em all. The improvements outside. The light gay kitchen, the curtains in the dining-room. The white sheepskin rug. Yes, I've seen all those. And I also saw you lose your temper, not with Scruffy, but with Jean –"

"She'd been out in the old bomb in the paddocks –"

"I know all about it –"

"Oh!" Rob's eyes narrowed. "Been telling tales already, has she?"

"She has not!" Pop's voice rose until it became almost a bull-like roar. "Her mother told me. Said you two are always at loggerheads – and if you carry on all the time in the same way as you did when she arrived back with Jack, then I don't wonder! What harm is there in driving the

146

bomb, may I ask? What right had you to stop her? I don't recollect saying she wasn't to touch it!"

"When you're away I'm in full charge here and what I say goes!" Rob shouted back.

"You," said Pop in a very crushing tone of voice, "are only the jackaroo on the property. Kindly remember it."

Rob got quickly to his feet and stared into the old man's eyes.

"Pop?" he asked slowly and questioningly, and at the anxiety in his eyes his foster-father's hand came down on his shoulder with a fierce pressure.

"Sorry, son," he apologised quickly. "I know what you're thinking. That wasn't what I meant at all." The alarm faded slowly from a face which had gone white under the tan. "To them you're only the jackaroo –"

"And they don't let me forget it," admitted Rob with a faint sigh of relief.

"And a jackaroo doesn't lose his temper with the boss's niece and lift her out of a car in the way you lifted Jean down. Wasn't surprised the dog flew at you. Served you right. In another minute she'd have done the same. Or would she?" Pop added thoughtfully under his breath.

"But she did!" Rob's hand moved against his cheek and he raised his eyes ruefully. "Sorry, Pop. I did forget myself out there. I hate being defied, for I'd warned her not to use the utility. So she promptly uses the other."

"No harm in it, son."

"I suppose that means she can have anything, any time?" Pop nodded. "In that case I want my own bus back," Rob said firmly.

"See no reason why not. Marie now wants to learn, then I suppose young Nigel will be nattering on the same subject."

"There's such an air of permanency about everything now," said Rob with a return of the moodiness. "They've done so much in the house and if they knew you could

147

afford it they would go on, upsetting every room and –"

"Making things so comfortable you'd never want to marry Valerie," finished Pop kindly. "I know. But if you aren't happy about what's happening, there's nothing to stop you marrying and leaving here if you want. I wouldn't hold you back – your happiness means a lot to me."

Rob looked at him suspiciously, mistrusting this sudden interest in his future. Then Pop changed the subject. "Got some presents for everyone. We'll find Nigel, have lunch – I'm hungry – then we'll open them all. But you have two things to do first." He stopped with his hand on the door-knob. "Get Marie to thoroughly cleanse that bite. Secondly, you will apologise to Jean – and don't look so mutinous about it either! I brought you up to be a gentleman –"

Rob gave in. He had to, for the tone of Pop's voice was a definite command, and grimly determined to get it over as quickly as possible, he went in search of Jean. He met her entering the hall and wondered at the sudden rush of colour over her cheeks as he stopped beside her.

"I want to apologise for what I did," he said stiffly. "It was a very ungentlemanly thing to do."

She raised her head uncertainly. "Thank you, Rob. And may I apologise for what I did? That was an unladylike action as well. Also for Scruffy. It was only because he's fond of me." She put her hand on his with a friendly little gesture. "Let's forget it, shall we?"

He nodded and turned to go in search of Marie, unwrapping the bandage as he did so, and slowly Jean walked back on to the veranda. The heavens had opened and it was raining hard, but the sound of it falling on the corrugated iron roof above her head and the sight of the wet ground outside only irritated her. No smile had accompanied his apology, she thought wistfully, and with a little sob she sank down on to the floor and put her arms round Scruffy, begging his forgiveness for the way she had scolded him. She knew he would have smiled at her if he had been able to do so, for his great brown eyes shone with devotion and his tongue licked the hair near her ear as his long tail thumped the floorboards ecstatically.

CHAPTER TWELVE

NIGEL gazed at the pile of gadgets for the kitchen, at Rob's new fishing rod and at the dainty work-basket which his sister was holding and then at the toys at his feet. There was a cricket bat, a decent one which should hit sixes, a real cricket ball – his mother had looked at this apprehensively and warned him not to play too near the house with it in case he broke a window – and some miniature cars. There were also a few more things guaranteed to please the heart of any boy. And Pop's reward was in his shining eyes.

"Gee, Uncle, thanks!" Nigel said more than once, lifting something up and fingering it, then putting it down again. "A pity it's raining," he said regretfully. "I would have liked to play cricket. You promised me a game." He looked at Rob and the young man nodded.

"We'll play as soon as we can," he promised. "Though it won't be much of a game with only two of us."

"Oh, Jean can play," answered Nigel casually. "She's a great slow bowler, and Mummy is good behind the wicket. We used to play on the sands when we lived in Melbourne. Let me look at all you've got, Mummy." He crossed the veranda and settled at his mother's feet, picking up an egg beater and whirling it round. "You must have been busy, Uncle. Where did you get the money to buy all these things?"

"Sold some sheep," answered Pop placidly, continuing to watch the rain. Rob had been right again and it was good to think some of the oats had been sown; this would germinate the seed very quickly, for the ground was still very warm.

"Couldn't you sell some more and buy a decent car?"

150

asked his nephew, poking his little finger in the holes of a fish slice.

Jean went hot and threw a despairing glance in her mother's direction. "It's not a car we need," she said gaily, pretending to be unconscious and unconcerned about her brother's bluntness. "It's some material."

"More curtains?" asked her brother-in-law.

"No." She turned in her chair. "Loose covers for the suite in the lounge I could make them easily, if we had the material." If Pop could afford to buy these toys, and she knew from past experience that they were not inexpensive, and if he could run riot in a hardware store and come home with all the gadgets which now lay about her feet just because he had sold some sheep, surely he could afford to buy the material they so desperately needed. There were still hundreds of sheep on the property and the lambing season was in full swing – hadn't she heard Rob say at lunchtime that nearly eighty per cent of the ewes now had lambs with them and that percentage was just a little higher than it had been last year? Two or three more who hadn't lambs could be sold and they would not be missed from the flocks, she reasoned, then she could have her loose covers.

Rob stood up and went to lean against the veranda post, gazing sombrely at the puddles which were forming on the path.

"What's wrong with the lounge suite as it is?" asked Pop awkwardly.

"It's very shabby," began Jean, and cast another glance at her mother. "We want to brighten up the room, and loose covers seemed the only solution. Obviously there's no need to buy a new suite, Uncle Gerald, the one in there is very solid and there are no springs gone, we've been over it all very carefully, but it does need something doing to it. Loose covers wouldn't be expensive."

"Hm!"

"Perhaps," Mrs. Delaney put her oar in, timidly, "you could give me an advance on the housekeeping. I know approximately how much I need each week now –" She stopped, biting her lips.

He turned his head to look at her. She was tucking away a stray lock of hair which had fallen over her forehead and she met his eyes appealingly.

"What's all the rush about?" he wanted to know.

"The Kennedys are coming for an evening very shortly, and I did want the house to look nice by then," she answered frankly. "And both Jean and myself are meeting more people, such pleasant people, and we will, I hope, be able to invite them all here in time –"

"Not getting snobbish, I hope," said Pop.

"Indeed, no!" Marie looked scandalised. "But this is such a stately kind of house, the rooms are so large and we could do much to improve them, without a great deal of expense. It hasn't cost you much so far, Gerald."

"No," he admitted cautiously.

"And it does look better, doesn't it?" Jean persisted.

He nodded, looking at Rob's straight back, guessing what the boy was thinking. There was an air of permanency about Marie's plans; she sounded as though she was going to live here for the rest of her life.

"Jean's birthday is in another three weeks," Mrs. Delaney said firmly, determined to say all she was thinking for once. Pop had not snapped at her or roared as he had roared at Rob during the afternoon, and things could not be so bad if he could bring home such a variety of gifts from the city. "I thought we could have another dinner party that evening."

"Can I stay up?" Nigel raised his head. "I like parties, especially Jean's, she thinks of such nice things to do and everyone doesn't sit round just talking all the time."

His mother nodded absently, still watching her brother-in-law's face, looking for some change in his expression which would tell her she was being thought too bold. and forward in her requests. The telephone rang shrilly at that moment and Rob turned, as though thankful something had come along to break up this conversation.

"It's Valerie," he called a minute or two later. "She wants to speak to you, Pop."

The old man heaved himself with a grunt from his chair, tweaked Nigel's hair as he passed and Marie sighed.

"She would ring now, just when I'd steeled myself to say all that and wanted a definite reply," she murmured ruefully, and Jean smiled at her sympathetically.

From the direction of the hall came a subdued muttering, then Pop shouted for Rob to return to the phone as Valerie had more to say to him and when he came back on to the veranda he looked down at his sister-in-law.

"Barbecue," he announced. "Valerie wants to have one out here next week. Said I told her it was all right. Did I?"

"Yes, you did say it," agreed Marie quietly. "The first night we were here."

"But –" Jean stood up with a frown on her forehead, "It's not Valerie who should be arranging barbecues out here, Gerald! Mother should do that! We don't want visitors until we've made those loose covers! And it's our home, not Valerie's, she should have asked Mother first if it was convenient." Her face was flushed and everyone looked at her in some surprise.

"Better tell her so," advised Pop.

"I will!" Jean swept into the hall and put her hand on Rob's arm.

"I want to speak to Valerie," she said clearly, and her uncle and mother exchanged glances.

Rob also glanced at her flushed face with surprise and with a muttered "Just a moment, Jean wishes to speak to you." He handed over the phone and leaned back against

153

the opposite wall with his arms folded. Jean's voice carried clearly on to the veranda.

"Valerie? My uncle has just told me of your desire to have a barbecue here next week –"

"That's right," agreed Valerie sweetly at the other end of the line. "I was going to come out and see him about it, but decided not to when it started raining. That track is a nightmare when it's wet, but it won't last long. Which day will be the most convenient?"

"No days at all for a while," said Jean firmly. "I'm sorry, Valerie, but we can't manage it at present. If you want a barbecue you must arrange it elsewhere."

"Oh! But Pop said –"

"He's been away and only returned before lunch, so naturally he doesn't know of any of the plans we've made."

"It was all arranged, Jean." There was a definite sharp note in the girl's voice, all the sweetness had vanished. "I told him I would do something about it – don't you remember? I've already asked quite a number of people I thought you would like to meet."

"There was some mention of a barbecue the evening we arrived," admitted Jean fairly. "But it was a vague arrangement and nothing definite was arranged. Later, perhaps, we'll do something about it, as such an idea is an agreeable one, but certainly not within the next few weeks. You'll have to tell your friends it's not convenient at present and cancel the plans you've made."

"Whatever will they think?" asked Valerie angrily.

"I'm sure they'll understand if you explain," said Jean in a steady voice. "My mother and I will send invitations to them all later when we have a party or some other entertainment. I'm sorry," she concluded, and handed the phone back to Rob, who had been listening with astonishment.

He held it away from his ear, unheeding the cries of, "Hello, hello, are you there?" and looking down into Jean's face. There was a defensive sparkle in her eyes and her

154

cheeks were rosy; she looked almost beautiful in her anger. She was up in arms against anyone coming to their home without first consulting her mother, and upsetting her. His face lost its moodiness and he smiled at her. Jean responded instantly and patted his hand gently as though begging his forgiveness for being rude to his friend.

Pop was also watching from the veranda; he had been listening as openly as Rob had done to the one-sided conversation and had quite made up his mind. Marie and Jean could have their loose covers – they were the first things they had asked for outright, covers to improve the appearance of the house, nothing for themselves. He would sell another sheep, he thought with an inward chuckle, then they could also have the linoleum for the kitchen. The rain appeared to be easing off and he decided to go outside again. Jean saw him move and received the impression that he was going out without referring again to their conversation. On the top step he turned.

"How old will you be, girl?" He shot the question at Jean and she merely stared. "Your birthday."

"Oh! Twenty-one."

"Hm. Quite grown up, aren't you?" There sounded to be an affectionate note in his voice, then his glance moved swiftly towards his sister-in-law. "I can manage a hundred dollars," he announced. "You'll have to make it go as far as you can."

"A *hundred*?" repeated Marie in a whisper, and Nigel whistled. That sounded like a fortune to him.

"That's all. You'll have to make it do." It was Pop's final word and he went down the steps, down the path and through the green gate.

"A hundred dollars!" breathed Marie unbelievingly, watching as Nigel bounded away after his uncle, his toys forgotten. "Why, I should have been happy with only half that amount!" She put her arm round her daughter's shoulders and drew her nearer. "We'll go into town and

155

make whoopee! Just think of all we can buy with a hundred dollars." Then her voice changed. "Dear, what's the matter? You've been very quiet since you came in just before lunch and even the thought of spending all that money doesn't seem to have awakened you from your dreams. You aren't worried or upset about anything, are you?"

"Of course not!" Jean hugged her mother, hiding her face against her shoulder. "I was out in the paddocks this morning, riding on a tractor and think I'm a bit stiff and sore as a result. It wasn't even as comfortable as the old bomb!"

"And that must be saying something! I thought you looked as though you'd had a shock." Marie tilted back the girl's head and looked lovingly into her eyes. "Sure there's nothing wrong?"

"Quite sure," said her daughter convincingly. "I think I'll have a bath –"

"Then lie down for a while. I'll get dinner ready, everything is prepared." Marie kissed the tip of the girl's nose and prodded her gently in the back. "Go along, child."

Jean was glad of the excuse to be alone for a while and leaving her mother humming gently and softly to herself as she gathered together the many gadgets which Nigel had scattered all over the floor, she went into the hall and hesitated. Rob was still leaning against the wall, one hand in his trousers pocket, occasionally nodding his head and saying, "Yes," or "No," and looking rather bored, and she could hear the faint mumble which was Valerie's voice.

"All right." He straightened himself as he saw Jean and put a definite end to the conversation. "I'll see you then. 'Bye."

The girl made as though to pass him, then looked questioningly into his face as he nodded towards the lounge.

"Did Pop tell you about the Show?" he asked in quite an affable tone leading the way into the room. "It's the annual event in the Creek and we are entering the usual

156

cattle and horses and I'm riding in a couple of events."

"That should be worth watching. When is it?"

"In about a fortnight's time." He wandered over towards the piano and she waited, wondering if he was going to try and play, but he seemed content to pick out a tune with one finger. "There's also a cooking competition and a flower show. Perhaps you would like to enter?"

"I'd love to. There are still plenty of flowers in the garden if you look under the weeds."

Rob nodded. "I'll mention it to your mother as well. Valerie thought you would like it."

"It was her idea, was it?" asked Jean, clenching her hands and remembering the lovely flowers and shrubs bordering the garden at Valerie's home.

"Yes, she usually enters something. She's riding one of the hacks, too."

And I hope she falls off! thought Jean viciously as she watched him. It was hard to believe he was in love with Valerie. He was such a curt tardy lover if the way he spoke to her on the phone was anything to go by, moody too; sometimes he was nice to her and sometimes he wasn't. Perhaps that was his attraction. And with me, thought Jean bitterly, he's nasty all the time. He was not a regular visitor to the Millers, calling only when requested to do so or whenever he happened to be in town, which was not often these days. He seemed afraid to leave the property, and she smiled to herself.

There seemed nothing else to say, so she left him still playing with one hand, up and down the ivories, musically not angrily, so perhaps Valerie had said something nice to him after her mother had made her declaration of independence.

That set Jean thinking. A dinner party for the Kennedys, that was all arranged and she would not have it altered. A birthday party – she creased her brows. Did she know people well enough to invite them to her twenty-first birthday? Or would it appear too obvious and forward? She must mention it to her mother and uncle and would abide by their decisions; perhaps these kind of things were looked upon differently in the country.

It rained on and off for two days and Jean became rather irritable. When she was angry with Nigel for some little thing he had done and which did not warrant a display of temper, her uncle looked at her from beneath his thick brows in a very disapproving manner.

"I'm sorry," she apologised both to him and to Nigel. "I admit I'm cranky. But this weather depresses me."

"Thought you liked rain?"

"I used to." She paused. "But the sun up here – it's so different and makes the whole world bright and cheerful. I also want to go into town to get that material. We haven't very long to plan and make up the covers and we can't go until the track dries out a little. I walked with Nigel down to the orchard yesterday and believe me, I was plastered with mud!"

"Oh, I can believe you," he said seriously. "You can drive into Dubbo when we go, there'll be more selection in the shops there."

"I can drive?" she smiled. "Oh, Uncle Gerald, how nice!"

"I'll go as well. Might as well see what you intend buying. You'll need a licensed driver with you. We'll leave Rob on the way. He has a car he wants to collect. His own –"

"The convertible?" asked Nigel eagerly. "Sam told me about it, says it's a beaut! I mentioned it to Rob and he nearly snapped off my head! Think Jean will be able to drive that too?"

Both his sister and his uncle looked at him and said simultaneously, "I'm sure she won't!"

"I didn't know he had a car," finished Jean suspiciously.

"Had one for years."

"Where has it been? And why has no one mentioned it before?"

"No concern of yours," retorted Pop.

She flushed, and walked into the house with her head held high.

They all found the wet days depressing, Nigel most of all because he could not go out with the frequency he was used to. Everywhere there was black mud after walking only as far as the cookhouse to talk to Sam made him either look piebald or like a blackfellow and his mother protested strongly because of the washing she could not get dry. So Nigel had to stay indoors and was given extra lessons which gave Marie less time in the house, so the bulk of the work and the cooking fell on Jean's shoulders. This was as good an opportunity as she would ever get in the kitchen and she began experimenting, telling Scruffy, who was always in constant attendance, that she would first try everything out on Uncle and Rob and if they survived and did not pass comments then she too would enter some delicacy in the cooking section of the show. Having had an excellent teacher in her mother she had a light hand with pastry and the fillings, as Rob remarked one evening with surprise, were "out of this world!"

That naturally encouraged her even more. If Rob was satisfied then a judge would be, and she branched out into other things with such success that Marie declared laughingly that she was resigning as cook and that her daughter could have the position.

"Like to go back to Sam's ideas?" asked Pop as he sat in the lounge one evening replete after a good meal.

"I would not!" It was a very definite reply and the old man chuckled.

"Changing your tune, aren't you, son?"

Rob passed his hand over his stomach and laughed. "Who wouldn't?"

There was a contented sigh from the opposite chair and Pop looked round the large room. He could see what Marie meant. The lounge suite certainly did want something doing to it; its dingy appearance spoilt the whole effect of the room, which despite the many flowers and the bits and pieces she had placed about, was too dark. The curtains had been displayed for his approval and in his mind's eye he could visualise them hanging by the large windows, and he nodded. The walls needed something doing to them as well; a couple of tins of that flat enamel would do much to improve matters, and he bit his lower lip thoughtfully. If Marie was given a free hand, both in the rest of the house and with his cheque book, why, no one would recognise Peppertree Lane.

"Must get one of the men in the garden," he muttered. "And buy some plants when we go shopping. Tell Ben to get cracking as soon as the soil is dry enough."

Feeling in his pocket for his pipe, he grunted; he had left it in his bedroom, so he heaved himself from the depths of the armchair and moved across the room.

"Pipe," he explained to Rob's look of inquiry. "Be back soon."

As he closed the door behind him he stopped. Scruffy was further along the hall, sitting on a doormat scratching behind one ear with a muddy black paw, Jean was in the kitchen washing up and she was singing softly. Marie was in the bathroom with her son, he could hear Nigel protesting loudly. "But *why*? I'd washed it yesterday!"

"You had your dinner yesterday too," replied his mother calmly.

"What's having my dinner to do with washing my neck?" asked the boy rebelliously, and Pop chuckled softly to himself. It all sounded so much like home, familiar sounds and voices blended into a family unit. He nodded. That was what they had become – a family, and they would stay like that until Rob made up his mind to marry Valerie.

The smile faded from his face. How dared that girl arrange a barbecue without first consulting either Marie or himself? It wasn't her home yet — he stopped halfway up the hall. If Rob married her would she come out here and take up the reins of the establishment? He had not thought of it from this angle before.

"No! Damn it, she won't!" he muttered.

For one thing, Marie would not stand for that, not now she was settling down and becoming in very truth the mistress of Peppertree Lane. For another thing, Valerie was too flighty. Never at home, always gadding round town and to Sydney for something or another. Thirdly, she was not much of a cook. Of the two he preferred Sam, he at least did give you something to eat. Valerie was all for lots of little courses, bits covered with parsley or olives or something else. No filling, he thought disgustedly. Not like Jean. Now that pie she had made for dinner was something a man could *eat*, especially when accompanied by a pile of well-cooked vegetables and followed by a — whatever did she call it? — and cream. Nice coffee, too. He opened the kitchen door wider and peered in.

"Any coffee left, girl?"

"Plenty," she smiled at him. "You want some more, do you?"

"Bring it into the other room."

He returned to the lounge, a bulky figure in untidy comfortable trousers and with a tieless shirt and wearing huge slippers. When she took in the coffee Jean looked at both men. They were so different, for Rob was lean and brown, he wore a collar and tie and his shirt sleeves were rolled neatly above his elbows, the muscles seemed to ripple under his skin as his arms moved. He was untidy with his belongings, but never with the clothes he was wearing.

"Nice to have a fire," murmured Pop as she put down the tray. "Good logs, those. Is your mother coming?"

"I'm here." Marie stopped by his chair; she had changed

161

her dress before dinner and wore a pale green jersey with a high neck for the little extra warmth needed in the evenings now, and he thought again what a slender figure she had for the mother of two and how neat she always looked.

"The boy in bed?"

"Yes, thank goodness!"

Rob played the piano for over an hour without getting up. He nodded his thanks when Jean took over a cup of coffee and placed it on top of the piano. It was still there, quite cold, when he finally moved away. Pop had three cups and relaxed in his chair with his eyes closed, Marie leaned her head back on a cushion and let the soft music dull her senses, and in the other armchair Jean was content simply to sit and watch Rob. She could only see the side of his face and his long hands as they flashed up and down the keys. When he did move and come towards the fire, rubbing his fingers, she smiled up at him.

"Thank you," she said very softly. "I enjoyed every note."

"You might have done, but it seems to have put the others to sleep!" He nodded towards the settee and the armchair. "Is there any coffee left?"

"I'm sorry, Uncle drank the lot. I'll make some more, but it will take a little time." She got to her feet and moved across to the door. Rob cast another glance at the two, who appeared to be sleeping soundly, put another log carefully on the glowing embers and followed her.

"We'll have it in the kitchen," he announced, quietly opening the door. "No need to wake them. Pop will probably want some more and he's had his share."

CHAPTER THIRTEEN

IT was doubtful who enjoyed the shopping expedition the most, Jean because she drove on the whole of the eighty-mile return trip and did not make a mistake even in the traffic of the busy western township which was their destination; Marie because she bought the material she wanted and many other things she needed besides with the money Gerald had given her; Gerald because he had not been shopping before with two women and he learnt many things, or Nigel who had an unexpected holiday from his lessons and added more to his own private zoo.

They left Rob in Murra Creek on a clear cold morning and Jean knew he had arranged to have lunch with Valerie. She tried hard not to think of it and did gradually forget as the old bomb bowled merrily along the tarred road past the open paddocks, many now green with young wheat or oats or lucerne, and the twisted gum trees, past the airport where they had made their first acquaintance with the West, into the streets where the traffic made her concentrate wholly on what she was doing and if she felt nervous she did not show it.

Marie surprised her brother-in-law in more ways than one during that long day. He stood beside her as she examined cretonne and brocades, listened as she discussed widths, lengths and prices with helpful assistants, then he pointed to one roll of material and announced firmly that that was his choice. She looked and shut her eyes.

"No," she said firmly. Who wanted wide stripes which looked more like veranda blinds?

"Then that one." He pointed to another roll and the next moment his sister-in-law's hands were on his shoulders, he was turned round and prodded in the back.

"Go elsewhere," she commanded. "You're useless here, Gerald. You've no taste and no idea at all what I have in mind! Please take Nigel and come back in about twenty minutes' time."

Obediently Pop did as he was told, to Jean's amusement, and that was how Nigel became the proud possessor of a small tank which contained tropical fish and which he had been admiring with great longing. Parcel after parcel was placed in the car and the old man scratched his head more than once as he wondered what they had purchased and how they had made a hundred dollars stretch so far.

Marie and Jean were both jubilant but confessed, as the warmth went out of the sun and the wind became cool during the afternoon, that they would be glad to return home, as their feet were aching with the now unaccustomed pavements. "They don't spring like soil," explained Marie seriously.

Peaceful was the word Jean used as they turned into the track near the house just on sunset. The countryside was quiet, settling down for the night, as were the beasts in the paddocks, and she for one was thankful for it. Her mother appeared to be looking round with appreciation and she smiled as they stopped at the gate. In another few months she would gradually make Peppertree Lane into a home they could all be proud of; it would have to be gradually unless Gerald could be persuaded to sell more sheep and make regular presentations. Rob was not there; he rang through later to say he was staying the night in town, a piece of information which made Jean press her lips together quickly.

After that the house became a hive of activity. Ben spent a morning in the garden digging over the flower beds and puddling in the many seedlings Pop had brought back with him. Bruce and Jack were brought in for a day to paint in the lounge, for Pop had refused point blank to allow either Marie or Jean to climb ladders and paint the ceiling, an

164

idea the men thoroughly agreed with, for it was a great change for them, and Mrs. Delaney was there regularly with the teapot and some of the delicious little cakes which put all Sam's efforts to shame. Jean was busy with the old sewing machine, stitching together the many pieces she had cut out with great care and giving the impression that she was surrounded and covered with gay colours and exotic flowers. Rob looked upon all that was happening without comment. He was preoccupied. Pop had emphasised that visitors, *any* visitors, were unwelcome at the moment. So to prevent Valerie driving out to find him as she threatened to do many times, accusing him of neglect Rob went into town more often in the evening. "At the time when he could have been making himself quite useful!" commented Jean to her mother.

Then came another burst of activity of a different kind on the property – the selection of the best sheep and cattle to represent Peppertree Lane at the show.

They were all happier here than they had ever been in the city. Both Jean and her mother found plenty to do and would find even more as time went on. They were planning cakes and fancy chiffon pies to enter in the show. Jean was crooning over rosebuds and ferns with the same idea in mind. Now the lounge was just as they wanted it, smelling rather strongly of new paint, but that would go in time, and Gerald had congratulated them upon their ingenuity so they were quite happy.

Nigel swung down from the saddle of his pony and smiled at his sister, who had wandered out to watch his efforts.

"You haven't been riding yet," he remarked.

"I've been too busy learning to drive," she answered.

"Aren't you satisfied now you have your licence?"

Jean smiled down into his face. "And how, sonny boy! It was so good of Uncle to go in with me, wasn't it? He never commented, though, when I came out and told him

I'd passed the test and was a fully fledged driver!"

"He took it for granted," said her brother. "A pity you can't drive Rob's convertible! Isn't it a beauty?"

His sister frowned. The red convertible was something she dared not touch. Its owner, in no uncertain manner, had made it quite clear that it was his car, only he had ever driven it, and it was very fast for anyone else who was not used to its behaviour and he would know, as surely as the sun rose each morning, if she had been near it. He was entitled to his own pleasures, she thought reasonably.

"Must have cost a lot," said Nigel thoughtfully, and she agreed. Jackaroos must get good money. Of course he was a bachelor and as far as she could make out he did not pay any expenses in the house, so naturally he must have saved it.

"Want a ride on Popski?" inquired the boy, and Jean looked at him doubtfully.

"Is he a hack?" she wanted to know, and he gave a peal of derisive laughter which made her cheeks redden.

"Don't you know what a hack is?" he asked.

"No." She shook her head. Valerie rode one, that was all she knew.

"Neither do I," remarked her brother, grinning, and she made a dart at him. He dodged and she chased him over the paddock until they were both hot and panting.

"Pax!" cried Nigel at last. "Pouf! You can run!"

"Physical fitness," she answered loftily. "Now I'll ride Popski home and have a rest."

He was smiling widely as she swung herself awkwardly up into the saddle. Her dress was not at all suitable for riding and stretched tightly above her knees. In vain she tried to pull it down and look more ladylike until Nigel told her briefly to leave it alone, there was no one here to see. She nodded, pulled the reins and Popski moved forward, disdaining the little extra weight.

What happened after that Jean never knew. Something

166

must have frightened him or maybe Nigel threw something at him, although she thought he had more sense than to do such a thing, and he never confessed to it, but the little horse suddenly swung away with a snort and galloped madly over the brown grass, refusing to take any notice at all of the voice behind his head telling him, pleading with him to stop and behave himself. The more Jean called, the faster he galloped. He had the bit between his teeth and made for the half open gate at the far end. Once through there he knew he had an open track. At the same moment as he rushed through the gate Rob came along in his car, and the sudden flash of red startled Popski even more and he was off like the wind.

Rob swore, did a wild turn, narrowly missing a large gum tree at the side of the track and set off in pursuit, wondering if Jean could manage to hold on until he reached her. If she was thrown when the horse was travelling at such a speed she could be seriously injured, and the dust was thrown up behind his wheels as he dodged trees and anthills, gradually nearing the river bank. The car swung on its chassis and the tyres screeched in protest as it was driven frantically nearer to the horse, who had the advantage of being able to leap over logs and dodge with great agility round trees. With the suddenness that he had started off on this mad gallop Popski stopped. He turned his head with its wild eyes and foaming mouth, neighed loudly and looked at Rob, who had come to a standstill with the same abruptness and was even now by his side.

"Jean!"

Very, very slowly the girl raised a white face framed by windblown curls and looked at him.

"Why, that's the first time you've ever called me by my name!" she gasped wonderingly.

Rob scowled. He had been expecting to find her half dead with fright and relieved at her rescue, yet all she could think of was that he had given her her rightful name.

"What were you doing?" he asked, holding tightly on to the reins. "Why are you riding Nigel's horse, and whatever did you do to make him bolt with you?"

"I didn't do anything." She was sitting limply in the saddle, afraid to get down because she knew her legs would crumple beneath her and somehow at this particular moment she felt she could not bear the exquisite pleasure of having him put his arm round her to hold her up. "He just set off and I had to come with him."

"You ought to have more sense – you can't ride – if I hadn't been near he might have thrown you down the bank!"

"If you hadn't come along just then he might even have stopped. You frightened him even more," she cried, on the verge of tears and fighting hard to keep them back, then she straightened herself and shook her head to make the curls go back into position, wishing her heart would stop this awful pounding against her ribs. "I want to learn to ride anyway," she finished with a touch of bravado.

"You want to do everything, don't you?" he asked angrily. "You're never satisfied. You'd better get down," he added more kindly as he noticed she was still white and that she was trembling. "I do wish you'd stop giving me heart failure. Every time I see you out here I wonder what you'll be doing next!"

Now you could take that two ways, thought Jean wisely. If he loved you it could be concern, but as he doesn't it's naturally anger. He wouldn't want to have heart failure in the paddock – whatever would Valerie say to that? She pushed her hair back again and wondered if she dared get down. Rob settled the question. One arm reached up, encircled her and pulled her out of the saddle. Scruffy was not here this time to witness the incident and show his disapproval.

"Don't do that," she gasped weakly, and against her will she sagged in his arms. Her legs felt like tissue paper and had not a bit of strength in them.

Rob glanced round. "Now, how are we to get home? You can't go back on Popski, he'll have to be watched, if this is what he's going to do Nigel had better not ride him again." He looked towards his car and his brows drew together.

"I don't want to." She moved from him.

"Don't want to what?"

"Drive that home!" She waved her hand towards the red convertible.

"Did I say I was going to let you drive it?" he inquired coldly.

"No," she admitted.

"But that's what you'll have to do." He scowled more fiercely than ever. No other person, not even Pop, had driven that car and he had had more than one argument with Valerie on the subject. For a moment he closed his eyes. "Go on, get in," he said roughly.

Jean obeyed because she knew she could not walk. She sat down limply behind the wheel and stared dumbly at the opposite side of the placid river where the gum trees grew thick and tall and reflected their graciousness on the water.

Then Nigel appeared with Pop by his side, running anxiously towards the couple on the bank, one in the car and the other still holding the errant horse.

"Jean!" Pop's voice was hoarse. "Are you all right, girl?"

"Of course she is," returned Rob shortly. "Perhaps this will teach her not to do things she doesn't know how to do!"

"Oh, you beast!" murmured Jean, wiping a tear away from one eye with a finger.

"What did you do?" asked Nigel, reaching his horse and patting him. "Did you frighten him or something?"

His sister sat upright in the driving seat and looked at him. "No, I did not," she cried emphatically. "You're all concerned about the horse, but only Uncle –" she held out her hand blindly and Pop rushed forward to put his arm round her shaking shoulders – "cares about me," she finished against his warm broad chest and he patted her soothingly and reassuringly.

"Go home, Rob," he ordered curtly. "And you, boy."

Nigel scrambled up on to Popski's back and Rob led them both away. Pop watched them out of sight and then he looked down at his niece's curly head resting so confidently against him.

"Get a fright, girl?" he asked gently, and she nodded. "Wobbly in the legs?" and again she nodded, but this time she raised her face with a tremulous smile round her lips.

"You know how it feels?" she asked hopefully.

"Too right! Horses have bolted with me before today. Been thrown many times. Bulls have also made me targets for assault and they've always left me with a queasy feeling in my tum and legs made of water."

"I thought of tissue paper," Jean laughed weakly.

"Same thing. Both useless as limbs." He tightened his arm round her. "So Rob let you in here, did he? Should feel honoured, girl. Now let's go home. The Kennedys are coming tonight, have you forgotten?"

He could not find a handkerchief, so wiped her eyes on the collar of his shirt, patted her again and went to sit beside her. With infinite care Jean drove back to the homestead and left the car at the gate where Marie, the picture of great concern, was waiting for her and her arms enfolded her immediately. She did not ask questions. Nigel had done his best to explain what had happened, but it had been such a long recital that she preferred to wait until her daughter had recovered for the shorter, and most probably the more truthful version.

Knowing how she enjoyed fussing over her, Jean let her do it and much later she leaned back against the pillows, her hair neatly brushed into place and wearing a gay dressing-gown, and laughed gently at her mother when she returned to the bedroom after a hurried visit to the kitchen.

"I'm all right now, dear," she answered the anxious look of inquiry. "It just shocked me at the moment. Then I had a further shock when Rob told me to drive his car back!"

"It could have been serious," said her mother reproachfully. "You mustn't ride again."

"There's a first time for everything," remarked her daughter, surveying her fingernails critically. "Perhaps this was a bad beginning, but it hasn't lessened my determination one bit about learning to ride."

"I'll speak to your uncle about it," was the only reply she received. "I must go, our visitors will be here shortly and the dinner must be just *so*! Get dressed, but don't rush dear, I've everything well under control and I left Gerald in the kitchen stirring the soup."

Jean stared after her as she walked across the bedroom and as the door shut she leaned back and closed her eyes. Uncle stirring soup! Oh, bless the man! What a comforting arm he had placed round her earlier in the afternoon, a gesture of affection she had rarely received from her own father. He disliked demonstrations as he called them. She smiled. It had been worth the shock to have Rob lift her down, even if he had done it so carelessly, and then to have uncle show his regard in the concern of his voice and subsequent actions. He was a dear, a big bulky lovable darling, she thought laughingly, with a bark far worse than his bite as her mother was beginning to discover. Stirring soup! That amused Jean very much, but not a hint of it showed on her face when she went into the kitchen and relieved him of the big spoon.

"All right?" he asked anxiously. "But of course you are!" He looked down at her flushed face and with a swift glance took in the gleaming curls, the lovely dress, and he found it hard to believe she made such things herself, and the neat shoes.

"Uncle, what's a hack?"

"Horse for general purposes. Why? Want one?"

"I'd like to learn to ride." She stirred the soup and cast a watchful eye over the other pans.

"Riding is going out of fashion these days, girl. Folk prefer cars. But there's no harm in being able to ride. Properly," he added with a twinkle in his eyes, and she laughed at him affectionately.

Jean, sniffing round the lounge as she waited for the visitors to arrive, decided the smell of new paint had quite disappeared and she was easy in her mind. The loose covers looked very new and had not received the sat-upon look she would have liked them to acquire – but oh, what a difference those and the paint, not to mention the curtains, made to this lofty room. A fire glowed welcomingly in the hearth, Pop was wearing a collar and tie for once and looked quite distinguished with his hair combed and tidy; Rob – well, Rob always looked handsome and well tailored, and even Nigel with his shining face and also wearing a tie with his little suit appeared to be on his best behaviour. He had been somewhat subdued by the sight of his sister being borne away across the paddock on his usual quiet little horse and was wondering now if his uncle would forbid him to ride Popski again.

A car was heard coming up the track. Mrs. Delaney patted her hair gently, smoothed down her dress and with a last glance round the cosy room she went towards the veranda to welcome her first official guest at Peppertree Lane. They came in smiling and Nigel immediately rushed Anne off to see his tropical fish. By the time he had finished the ice was well and truly broken, sherry was being passed round and the three men were standing before the fire with their hands behind their backs talking earnestly together.

Anne Kennedy almost crooned over the covers which Jean had made with such painstaking care and said so emphatically and sincerely. She admired the curtains and sur-

172

veyed the newly painted walls with such open interest that her husband laughingly told her it was bad manners to stand about and stare so. But after dinner Jean discovered him in the kitchen with Gerald, who was displaying the cream and red cupboards and the cheeky curtains with great pride and she crept away before they noticed her, a laugh in her eyes.

It was only to be expected that Rob should entertain them at the piano, and it was discovered that Anne had a pleasant contralto voice, and before long all of them were grouped round Rob singing lustily and thoroughly enjoying themselves. Then the telephone bell rang and a silence fell upon them all. Rob got slowly to his feet.

"Valerie," he muttered, and went from the room.

There was a brief conversation and then the receiver was slammed back on its hook. When he re-entered the lounge the Show was the main topic of conversation, and Mrs. Kennedy confided she was entering orchids in the non-competitive section of the flower show. Jean looked at her.

"Orchids?"

"My hobby. It's difficult growing them here, as the summers are so hot, but I do get a few blooms. Before you leave for the show, Jean, I'll send you a spray."

"You're a dear, and I shall love them," said Jean warmly. "I've never had orchids before."

Pop changed the subject. "So you like our alterations," he said, taking some of the credit for what had been done, before their visitors departed. "Think we're going to have some more."

Marie raised her eyebrows. "Are we?"

"We are."

"Where?"

"All over the joint. New bath. That one's had its day. Shower recess. Alter the wall, built in alcove – seen one in a magazine somewhere. New oven –"

173

"No," said his sister-in-law flatly, "I don't want a new oven."

He looked across at her. There was a light of battle in her eyes and she seemed to have forgotten the other four people in the room.

"Why? That's worn out too –"

"It is not! It's a good oven and I won't have it changed!"

"Mutiny!" cried Pat Kennedy with his slow smile.

"Definitely," agreed Jean, looking at her mother with respect.

"I am not being mutinous," contradicted Marie. "But I am now used to that oven. We've grown to understand each other and as long as the men keep me supplied with wood I shall continue to use it. Do you understand, Gerald?" Her cheeks were flushed. She should not be putting her foot down so forcefully in front of her guests, but they were such natural people who were obviously used to saying what they thought and so would not think it strange. She hoped not. And where was Gerald getting the money to make these proposed alterations, she would like to know? Selling more sheep? If that was the case she could think of many other things needing alteration too.

Gerald shrugged his shoulders helplessly as if to say you couldn't argue with a woman and gave her the victory.

"If you say so, Marie."

Jean looked from her face to that of her uncle. So Marie had found her feet at last! In future she would rule the homestead and its occupants and they would bow to her wishes.

CHAPTER FOURTEEN

THE show was scheduled to last two days, during which time Murra Creek was on holiday. There was a circus and many sideshows, and these, as Pop explained seriously as he handed some money to Nigel, arrived for the sole purpose of entertaining little boys and he could visit them all. There were two large halls filled with exhibits from the surrounding countryside: wheat, wool, everything else from paint and furniture to home-made scones and jars of pickle. Then in the ring were the entrants for the various riding events, the judging of cattle and the wonderful Grand Parade.

Jean drove in very early by herself on the first morning and feeling rather nervous among many busy women, placed her exhibits with the numerous others in the great hall. Her baskets and sprays of flowers looked rather paltry she thought as she rearranged them for the last time. The selection of blooms at Peppertree Lane was not very large, and the sponge cakes, Marie's entry, appeared a trifle flat to her jaundiced eyes. Then she bumped into Rob as she was leaving and for the second time he surprised her with a smile.

"Finished everything?"

"Yes, they're all there, but with so many others I'm sure the judges will overlook mine!" she confessed, and looked him up and down. "You look very grand."

He was wearing a riding outfit and appeared taller than ever, then she realised she was wearing low-heeled shoes which helped the delusion.

"What are you going to do now?"

"Drive home again." The thirty-two-mile return trip did not worry her nowadays. "Uncle said there was little doing during the morning and as there were a few things he had to attend to he preferred to come after lunch."

"I'll see you all then. Be in early." He smiled and hurried away and the girl thought that his haste was because he had seen Valerie, who was in the distance near the grandstand with her mother. For a moment she watched, saw Valerie run forward and thrust her hand through Rob's arm with a possessive little gesture and laughingly turn to her mother with some remark. Jean did not wait to see any more, but ran back to the car, put it in gear and drove out of the gates with such a speed that the police constable on duty looked twice at the rapidly disappearing vehicle. He knew what it was and who it belonged to and shrugged his shoulders; he must have been mistaken, for Pop Delaney's old bomb had not topped thirty miles an hour for many a year.

After an early lunch Marie, poised and serene, led the way from the house and paused by the side of the ancient car.

"This totally spoils the whole effect," she announced, glancing down at her tailored suit with its delicious fluffy little blouse. Jean stopped beside her and Pop pulled up suddenly to avoid bumping into her. "Don't you think so, Gerald?"

"Done me for a long time," he observed mildly.

"Now it's had its day. We need a new one," she stated calmly.

"And how!" murmured Nigel.

"Well now!" Pop stepped forward, looked at the car and at his relations. Both Jean and her mother were wearing beautiful clothes, even he knew that, and he was proud he belonged to them, or that they belonged to him, and he was ready to accede the point about the conveyance letting them down. He stroked his chin and his eyebrows appeared to slip further down over his twinkling eyes. "What do you suggest we do about it?"

176

"We can't do anything at the moment." Marie scrambled carefully into the back seat, her usual place, and was surprised when he got in beside her. Nigel made a beeline for the front to be with his sister; it would not be long before he coaxed Jean to let him try to drive on his own.

"I think we can," Pop continued the conversation as they moved away from the house and his sister-in-law looked at him.

"Are you thinking of selling more sheep?" she inquired sweetly.

For a moment he looked dumbfounded. Nigel spun round to peer over the back of the seat and Jean glanced quickly into the driving mirror, her mother still looked poised and her eyes were dancing with mirth.

"Y-yes," stuttered Pop, laughter bubbling in his throat, both at her effrontery and the fact that she had hit upon the truth. There were those ewes in one of the far paddocks, he had heard of someone who wanted them, for they were pure-bred merinos. The laughter threatened to choke him and he could not keep quiet any longer. Guffaws of mirth sounded through the trees and he slapped his knees and his shoulders were shaking.

"Oh, Marie!" he did manage to speak at last. "You aren't as silly as I thought you were!"

"You did think that once, didn't you?"

"Sure. After living with Fred all those years I thought you must be." He patted her arm to take away any offence from the words. "But you aren't."

"No," she replied quietly, "I'm not."

He sobered down and wiped his face on a spotlessly clean handkerchief.

"So you've guessed, eh?"

She nodded. It had not been difficult. She read the papers, listened to the bulletins for farmers on the radio, and she had heard him speaking to Rob about sending sheep away to the sales and she knew that with the high prices those sheep brought to the men who had sent them there the cheques would not be small ones. There was also the wheat and the fruit and those mysterious wool cheques she had heard others mention during conversation. Also she knew that neither Pop or Rob would work as hard as they did or buy the very latest in farming machinery and equipment if there was to be nothing in return for their labours.

"Why did you do it, Gerald?" she asked, knowing perfectly well that neither of her children could follow this conversation. Nigel couldn't and she had seen the frown on Jean's face.

"Tell you later," and he nodded towards the front seat. "No need for you to be offended, Marie. It was done for a purpose."

"You wondered whether we could stay the course, didn't you?"

He gave her an admiring glance. "Got all the answers, haven't you?"

"I hope so," she answered serenely, and smiled.

"You're not mad at me for playing a trick on you?" he asked pleadingly.

"No."

"And you'll stay?"

"If you want us to, yes," she said quietly and steadily.

"I do," he cried devoutly, and settled back with a sigh of content.

Jean could have a new car for her twenty-first birthday. He would walk her through the displays this afternoon and find her preference. Nigel could go to college in another couple of years, the same college Rob had attended, and Marie could go ahead with all the alterations she wanted in the house. It was to his benefit in the long run anyway, and surely after all these years he was entitled to some comfort and relaxation? Rob could attend to the property; once Nigel was at school he might take Marie round Australia and show her the sights. She would be a good companion now she had lost her fear of him. He glanced at his niece. Couldn't leave her alone to look after Rob while he went gallivanting with her mother. Wasn't the thing. He would have to think of something, but there was plenty of time.

Most of the afternoon was spent in the grandstand watching the various riding events and Jean's hands tightened on her lap when she saw Valerie riding a beautiful brown horse. It held its head high and stepped out with pride as though exhibiting itself before all the spectators was its life's work. Valerie was sitting upright, a neat figure in her habit, and Jean sighed. Never would she be able to ride like that. She was too small and would be lost in the saddle! No wonder Rob had so much in common with the girl; he too was a magnificent horseman.

"Doesn't she look funny wearing that bowler hat?" asked Nigel.

"Hush!"

"But doesn't she? I hope you never wear one." Then a few minutes later, "She's changed horses. Why? What's she showing off for?"

"She isn't showing off," whispered his sister frantically, for his clear young voice carried. "She's riding in another event."

"Oh! I wonder how many more horses she's got? I've only one." He pointed quickly. "Look, there's Mrs. Kennedy! And she has a bowler hat on too," he added with distaste. "Oh, she's got the ribbon!" and he clapped enthusiastically and waved when he thought Anne was looking towards them and behind him Mrs. Miller looked down her nose at the back of his bare head.

Jean caught her uncle's eye and nodded to her brother; he nodded back and decided they would leave – more interesting things awaited elsewhere. With a sigh of relief Nigel went down the steps and once in the pavilion he promptly lost himself.

A second prize, thought Jean, was decidedly better than nothing, and she looked at the card before her basket of flowers with pride. Further away a first prize had been awarded to Miss Miller, but that was understandable. Valerie had been entering shows for years and had a good idea what the judges looked for in the exhibits, also she had a beautiful garden with hundreds of blooms to pick from.

"Congratulations," said a voice behind her, and she spun round to find Rob at her elbow. "You did very well considering it was the first time. Your mother has got a champion ribbon for her sponge cake."

"I expected that." Jean looked pleased. "Her cakes are —"

"Out of this world. Yes, I know." He laughed and her heart gave a little lurch of happiness. "Have you been round the pavilion yet?"

"I came in with Nigel and lost him, then I made for the flowers to see what had happened. I shall treasure that card."

"It will probably be the first of many," he said, leading her away. "Your orchids look nice."

She glanced at the spray on her coat and flushed. "It was very good of Anne to send them when she must have been so busy."

"They've been lucky at Gum Valley," said Rob thoughtfully. "Pat won the champion ribbon for a bull and has six firsts in other classes. We have an invitation to go there on Sunday."

She liked the sound of that "We have an invitation." It did not sound remote or cold and she trembled a little at the touch of his hand under her elbow. He led her round all the exhibits, giving explanations when she asked for them and pointing out all he thought would be of interest. Nigel was eventually discovered looking at a display of honey and wanted a comb, but when informed that it was for display only he tucked his hand in his sister's and dragged along behind. Rob stopped two or three times and introduced Jean to people he knew. She was greeted by some of the ladies she had met at the tennis club and was the centre of a small group by the door when Valerie and her mother came in.

"Oh, Rob, there you are!" exclaimed the girl brightly. "I've been looking everywhere for you. Hullo, Jean," as her eyes moved swiftly, taking in everything Jean wore from head to toe. "How *nice* for you to win that second!"

"I was very pleased about it," Jean smiled. "How are you, Mrs. Miller?"

"Very well, thank you. What delightful orchids!"

"Aren't they? Mrs. Kennedy sent them over early this morning."

"They're a glorious colour," said a woman standing by Mrs. Miller's side.

"They're more suitable for an evening dress," remarked Valerie coldly.

"But exquisite!" said her mother, having another close look.

"They've no pong," announced Nigel.

Jean's face flushed a brilliant scarlet with embarrassment and Rob laughed outright, his whole face crinkling with amusement. Mrs. Miller looked at him with hauteur and turned away.

"What a horrible child!" she remarked before she was out of earshot. "Is that the brother?"

Rob's face changed its expression, his lips narrowed to a thin line and his eyes, as they followed Mrs. Miller's progress into the crowd, were cold with dislike. Valerie, who had been grabbed tightly by the arm, flashed him an appealing glance before she vanished from sight round the cake stands.

"Did I say something wrong?" asked Nigel innocently, glancing first at his sister and then at Rob.

"Oh, Nigel!" she breathed. What else could she say?

The orchids had little perfume, that was quite true, but what a way to put it! "Wherever did you learn that expression?"

The boy glanced up at the man standing so stiffly by his side. "From Rob. He said the fowlyard ponged –"

This time it was Jean who laughed; she did so helplessly, otherwise she felt she would have cried. She and Nigel had let him down in front of Valerie and her mother, would he ever forgive either of them for what had happened she wondered dully.

"I think I'll find Uncle," she said in a stifled voice, and Rob nodded.

"Yes, do." He also vanished from sight round by the cake stands and when she next saw him in the distance, he was near the car park talking to Mrs. Miller.

Pop enjoyed himself after Jean and Nigel came rushing to his side as though seeking his protection. He listened to the girl's halting explanation of the way they had offended Mrs. Miller, he gripped her shoulder and tweaked Nigel's hair, telling them not to worry, Mrs. Miller was not by any means everyone in Murra Creek and Mrs. Kennedy had been looking for the boy to show him a Shetland pony – would he like to try and find her? Nigel was off like a shot from a gun, totally unrepentant. Then Pop glanced down at his niece's woebegone face.

"Forget that old hag," he advised, "and come with me. Something here I want you to look at." He led the way towards a display of well known English cars. "Like one of 'em?" he asked, and Jean thought he was trying to take her mind off what had happened and entered willingly into his gay pretending mood.

"Oh, definitely!" she cried as though choosing a car was an everyday occurrence. "The little one, I think, it's just my size!" She pointed to a small blue sedan and he walked across and opened the door. The interior was upholstered in fawn and looked very comfortable.

"Get in."

She slipped behind the wheel, settling herself in the bucket seat, fingering everything and wistfully thinking that this was just her weight, for it was small and compact, and she could handle it easily and feel very much at home in it. Imagine the joy of driving to Murra Creek, to Gum Valley and to other places in the comfort of her own car! Pop watched her.

The sales man, who was also the demonstrator, came bustling over when he saw their interest. "Hello, Pop! Going to buy your niece a car, eh? Why not try it out, Miss Delaney," he tempted her, and she could not resist.

"Can I?"

"Of course! I'll come with you, get in the back, Pop, you might as well have a free ride and see how they both behave!"

Two minutes later Jean was driving round the outskirts of the showground, revelling in the feel of the little car under her hands. Pop's eyes were on the back of her head, loving, kindly eyes and he leaned over her shoulder.

"Like it?"

"Oh yes!" She could not keep the longing out of her voice.

"You handle it beautifully. O.K. Aub, we'll have it — hey, steady, girl! Mind the fence post!"

She came to a sudden stop and spun round in her seat. "Oh, Uncle, don't tease me," she pleaded. "I've had enough today —" her voice broke a little.

"Not teasing you, girl," he said gruffly. "I'll buy this for your twenty-first birthday. That's what I'll do."

"B-but —" wide-eyed, she stared at him. "You can't afford it!"

Aub, the salesman, laughed. "Don't you believe that tale, Miss Delaney! In fact, he's rolling in it. He absolutely —"

"Pongs!" murmured Jean a trifle hysterically, and

clutched the hand gripping her shoulder. "Oh, *Uncle!*"

"Better drive it back yourself, Aub," advised Pop. "She ain't fit. Shock, you know," he added kindly.

In a daze Jean listened to the exchange of banter as Pop calmly wrote out a cheque and she stood near him, frightened he might suddenly vanish and leave her. Aub placed a large "Sold" notice on the windscreen of the tiny car and smiled.

"Let me come to your party, won't you, Miss Delaney? We must christen this!"

"Of course you must come. Your wife too – if you're married." She turned away. "Uncle, I don't know what to say or how to say it. I thought you were having such a struggle to make ends meet, I'm sure you can't really afford it. You're just being nice to me." He shook his head smiling. "Oh, I shall wake up in a minute and find I've been dreaming!"

"You're awake, girl. I wanted to see you all settle at Peppertree Lane, if you could, to coin your mother's phrase, stay the course. I'm happy because you've done so. Don't want to return to Melbourne, do you?"

"Never! Oh, you are a dear!" Unheeding the many people around she reached up and kissed his cheek, then tucked her hand under his arm. "Where is Mother? I must tell her! Does she know you aren't as destitute as you pretended to be?"

"She knows. She guessed. I've quite a bit of dough," said Pop modestly. "Might as well spend some of it now, can't take it with me when I die. Marie is watching the demonstrations of a number of washing machines, she wants one in the laundry. Evidently she likes the oven but hates the big fuel copper. Let's go and find her."

"And seeing Jean is to have a car," cried Nigel enviously as they drove home, "can I have a bike,"

"Probably."

"And do you think I could have a –"

184

"Nigel!" cried his mother sternly, and as she looked at him he subsided into a sulky silence.

"Where's Rob?" asked Marie as she entered the hall which was in darkness. The house was quiet, the surrounding countryside was peaceful and she gave a sigh of thankfulness to be home again.

"With Valerie, I suppose," answered her daughter quietly. Perhaps he was still apologising for the vulgar expression Nigel had used.

"I am *not*! I'm here." Rob followed them in smiling "I've been trailing home in your dust –"

Pop looked at him from beneath the bushy eyebrows. "Not like you to trail anyone, son. Usually you pass everything. Car gone bust or something?"

"No sense in getting home first when there was no one here to welcome me. Hope everyone enjoyed the show? And you're all going again tomorrow?"

"Too right!" cried Nigel, and his mother and sister nodded.

Jean unpinned the lovely orchids and held them in her hands for a moment. Perhaps they had unwittingly caused the end of any hopes she might have had. Rob would have had to make much of Mrs. Miller to coax her back into a good humour, when she walked away she looked so cold, icy and aloof. If she was to be his mother-in-law – oh, heaven help him! She thought suddenly, and ran towards her room to take off her hat and coat.

A cold meal had been left in the refrigerator and afterwards Marie announced that she felt like playing a game of billiards and Pop followed her into the room as Nigel went to fetch his train set. Rob drifted off into the lounge and Jean could hear him at the piano; the music was not loud or angry, it was soft, soothing, just what her jaded nerves needed, so she crept quietly into the room hoping he would not see her and curled up in one of the large chairs where she could watch his face. As he continued playing she

185

thought of the little car she was to collect after the show, of the washing machine her mother had purchased and the many things her uncle had promised to let them do in the house. She tried to think of everything but Rob, Valerie and Mrs. Miller.

"So she has a little car of her own," he remarked softly, and she started. He did not look angry, on the contrary he seemed more relaxed than he had done for weeks and he was smiling as he played.

"Oh! I was hoping you wouldn't hear me come in. I didn't want to disturb you."

"You didn't disturb me. But despite all the things your mother did in this room she forgot to oil the hinges of the door."

"I've never noticed," said Jean.

"No. It was just one of those things you connect with home, wasn't it? Like the gate, the squeak that never bothered me until it was no longer there."

She glanced at him swiftly and smiled at the recollection.

"Now Pop has spilt the beans and told you he's not a poor man –"

"Yes." She started fiddling with the clasp of her belt. "But it won't make any difference at all, excepting that we can go on making the house more comfortable for all of us."

"That idea doesn't suit me." He went on playing, his foot pressed down on the soft pedal.

"You can always leave here if you wish," she replied rather stiffly. "We know perfectly well that we haven't pleased you by doing all we have done. But as long as Uncle is satisfied that's all that matters!"

His fingers ran up and down the keys. "Naturally. He's a wonderful person."

"I know." Her voice softened.

"And I know better. He didn't tell you that he brought

186

me here when I was a child, did he? My mother died soon after I was born, my father a few years later, and Pop, because he had loved the woman who was my mother, his Elizabeth as he's always called her, brought me to Peppertree Lane and looked upon me as his son –"

"Oh!" Jean's face was scarlet. "Is that true?"

"Ask Pop if you don't believe me." Still he went on playing, drifting from one gentle melody to another.

"But I thought – we all thought you were the jackaroo."

He inclined his head gravely and desperately she wished she could see his face. "So you told me, many times."

"I'm sorry," she whispered. "We butted in on your companionship, and I was rude to you, but I didn't know. I merely thought you rather aggressive – how you must hate us for all we have done!"

"I did hate the thought of you coming here," he confessed. "When you came I hated the idea of you putting up curtains, painting cupboards, oiling gates and doing so many other things. It looked so permanent. Then, when I'd got used to all that, I hated the idea of you driving round the paddocks in the old bomb, a car which had long since had its day and which might collapse at any moment, the steering might have given way when you were passing between trees, the brakes might have failed to respond when you were near the river bank. I hated the idea of you riding horses, because you're such a tiny little thing and horses are immensely strong. I hated seeing you on Popski, hanging on for dear life as he brushed against those gate posts –"

Jean was standing up, becoming aware at last that the tune he was playing was "I Dream of Jeannie with the Light Brown Hair."

"Rob!"

"I'm silly, aren't I, to have flutters like that, at my age too! Other women drive, ride, do all kinds of things, but mostly they're big tall women and they're all other women, they're not *you*!"

187

"Rob!"

"You're so small and dainty," and he played the tune again and she knew, as she stood there, that she would remember it and love it all her life. "Jeannie," he said softly, and spun round on the chair to look at her at last.

"I'm not staying in this house," he announced, holding out a hand and timidly she placed hers in it and felt it tighten with warmth and strength. "I'm going to build another house nearby and there, if you're willing, you can put up more curtains, paint more cupboards and doors, plan kitchens and bathrooms to your heart's content. You can also make meat pies that melt in my mouth and fruit cakes that are full of cherries – sweetheart, don't look at me like that! I'm just warning you now that that's what I'm going to ask you to do, when you've become used to the idea of having me around all the time without anyone else in tow –"

"Valerie?" she whispered, standing by his side and letting her free hand rest gently on his hair.

"That's all finished with." His jaw hardened for a moment. "I never loved her, never. Understand? I've finished with the Millers. I knew the break had to come and it did this afternoon. Nigel started it with his remark –" he laughed up into her face. "Then I followed them and heard in no uncertain terms all they thought about him, you, and the rest of us at Peppertree Lane. It wasn't very nice – both Valerie and her mother forgot for a short time that they were supposed to be ladies! As a mother-in-law I must prefer Marie."

She looked down at him and her face softened, became welcoming, loving and confident and Rob drew in his breath deeply and got to his feet, catching her in his arms as he did so.

"Jean?" he lingered over her name, hesitatingly, hardly daring to believe what he was seeing in her eyes and on her face. "Sweet, do you think you could soon get used to the

:dea of having me around for always? For ever?"

"I think so." She found she only reached up to his shoulder, an ideal position as she could rest her head there so comfortably. "I've had you around for quite a while now and have become used to you, you're rather nice – Oh, Rob, I don't think there's any need at all for you to wait about much longer!"

"Then you'll marry me and live with me in a house we'll build –"

"At the other end of Peppertree Lane –"

They stopped to look at each other again and his arms tightened still more round her slim figure.

"You adorable little scrap!" he muttered thickly, and bent his head to kiss her.

Mills & Boon's Paperbacks

APRIL

UNWANTED BRIDE BY ANNE HAMPSON

Caryn and Sharn had made a marriage of convenience and she hadn't seen him since the wedding. Now she needed his help – but would he be willing to give it?

FAIRWINDS BY REBECCA STRATTON

Tara was sure she loved her fiancé Clifford. So why did she find his brother Philip so intriguing?

THE RED PLAINS OF JOUNIMA BY DOROTHY CORK

'Skye Bannerman's an ogre,' someone had told Pippa – and she quite agreed. But perhaps he had a more attractive personality to show to the sophisticated Angela Glas.

DARK ANGEL BY ELIZABETH ASHTON

Would Francesca ever understand her enigmatic husband Angelo? Could she ever love him?

STORMY ENCOUNTER BY ROUMELIA LANE

Jane was worried on her mother's behalf and went out to Ibiza to sort things out – but only managed to fall foul of Bruce Walbrook.

GALLANT'S FANCY BY FLORA KIDD

Sweet-talking Roger Gallant was part of Miranda's job – but how well could she manage to do it?

THE BENEDICT MAN BY MARY WIBBERLEY

Beth was looking forward to working for nice Mrs Thornburn – until she realised that it was really David Benedict who required her services, and he was not quite so nice as his aunt!

SILVER FRUIT UPON SILVER TREES BY ANNE MATHER

Sophie hadn't taken long to fall in love with Edge St. Vincente. But she was in Trinidad under false pretences, and Edge thought she was his niece. . . .

DESERT NURSE BY JANE ARBOR

Nurse Martha Shore had needed a change, but hadn't she only jumped from the frying pan into the fire?

THE FEAST OF SARA BY ANNE WEALE

A romantic story set in the strange and lonely Camargue region of France.

20p net each